/808.3   Hoke, Helen   cop.3
          Thrillers, chillers, & killers.

D1443544

THRILLERS CHILLERS & KILLERS

Also edited by Helen Hoke

Eerie, Weird and Wicked
Demons Within
Ghostly, Grim and Gruesome
Spooks, Spooks, Spooks
Terrors, Torments and Traumas
Weirdies, Weirdies, Weirdies
Witches, Witches, Witches

ELSEVIER/NELSON BOOKS
New York

An Anthology by HELEN HOKE
THRILLERS CHILLERS & KILLERS

808.3
cop. 3

No character in this book is intended to represent any actual person; all the incidents of the stories are entirely fictional in nature.

Library of Congress Cataloging in Publication Data
Main entry under title:

Thrillers, chillers and killers.

CONTENTS: Nolan, W. F. Dead call.—Swoboda, N. C. Christopher Frame.—Counselman, E. The huaco of Señor Peréz.—Woollcott, A. Moonlight sonata.—Collier, J. Evening primrose.—Benson, E. F. The step.—Turner, H. Shwartz.—Riddell, Mrs. J. H. The old house in Vauxhall Walk.—Bradbury, R. The emissary.—Sansom, W. Various temptations.—Peattie, E. W. The grammatical ghost.—Derleth, A. The patchwork quilt.—Brown, F. Nightmare in yellow.
  1. Ghost stories, American. 2. Ghost stories, English. I. Hoke, Helen.
PZ1.T413 [PS648.G48] 813′.0872 79-4502

ISBN 0-525-66633-8

Published in the United States by Elsevier/Nelson Books, a division of Elsevier-Dutton Publishing Company, Inc., New York. Published simultaneously in Don Mills, Ontario, by Thomas Nelson and Sons (Canada) Limited.

Printed in the U.S.A. First Edition
10 9 8 7 6 5 4 3 2 1

Acknowledgments

Acknowledgments

"The Grammatical Ghost," by Ella Wilkinson Peattie. Reprinted by permission of Macmillan Publishing Co., Inc.

"The Huaco of Señor Peréz," by Mary Elizabeth Counselman. Reprinted by permission of Arkham House Publishers, Inc., Sauk City, Wisconsin.

"Moonlight Sonata," by Alexander Woollcott. From *The Portable Woollcott.* Copyright 1946 by The Viking Press, Inc. All rights reserved. Reprinted by permission of Viking Penguin, Inc.

"Nightmare in Yellow," by Fredric Brown. From *The Best of Fredric Brown.* Copyright © 1977 by Elizabeth C. Brown, Executrix of the Estate of Fredric Brown. Reprinted by permission of the author's agents, Scott Meredith Literary Agency, Inc., 845 Third Avenue, New York, NY 10022, USA.

"The Patchwork Quilt," by August Derleth. From *Over the Edge.* Reprinted by permission of Arkham House Publishers, Inc., Sauk City, Wisconsin.

"Shwartz," by Harry Turner. Reprinted by permission of the author and his agents, London Management.

"The Step," by E. F. Benson. Reprinted by permission of the Estate of the Late E. F. Benson.

"Various Temptations," by William Sansom. From *The Stories of William Sansom.* © William Sansom 1963. Reprinted by permission of Elaine Greene Limited.

Contents

About this Book

IT WAS WITH PARTICULAR DELIGHT that I gathered the present stories into what I believe to be an indispensable companion to my previous selections for the avid reader of spine-tingling tales.

Perhaps the most notable feature of this collection is its wide variety of highly diverse and striking stories by a distinguished list of authors, each of whom spin their own inimitable style of storytelling into a uniquely different pattern.

Something ghastly, disturbing, or frighteningly puzzling—something for everyone—is the keynote of this collection. There is a very evil, sickly-greedy man, whose diabolical scheme to achieve financial freedom turns out all wrong, to his infinite dismay and ultimate downfall; then, on a more tender note, a young girl is often warmly tucked into bed by loving hands long dead.

In a more contemporary fashion, a congenial fellow telephones an old friend to revive memories of the good old days when he was on earth. This is *the* story to remember whenever your phone rings! But you will find unforgettable the funny, yet somehow poignant, story of a loving couple in the midst of a most weird and variegated group of ghosts carrying on their everyday eerie business as usual.

One of the most memorable combinations you may

9

ever encounter is that of humor and horror—as skillfully portrayed by Harry Turner in "Shwartz." He will tickle your fancy and touch your heart—but this man-made monster will also have you trembling when he demonstrates his catastrophic, superhuman powers.

In the masterful hands of Mrs. J. H. Riddell, speaking to you from another time—indeed, from another century—you can shiver in empathy through a night's anguish as you settle down in "The Old House in Vauxhall Walk." Here, with the son of a wealthy admiral, your nerves may stretch to their utmost and tingle with the strange and fearful apparitions which make his sleep a nightmare.

The prolific and always ingenious Ray Bradbury will surely delight the hearts of all readers with his enchanting story about a boy and his *very* remarkable dog. This super-inquisitive canine—with a talent for digging up more than an occasional bone—unearths a most extraordinary treasure indeed. Enjoy the captivating suspense as you follow "The Emissary" on one of his nocturnal explorations into the unknown.

Imagination running wild is employed as William Sansom lures you down the back streets of London's Victoria district in search of a sadistic strangler. This gripping tale of terror might well serve as a brutal reminder to all young women to approach the "Various Temptations" of life with extreme caution.

Among the stories set forth in this collection, there undoubtedly is one—or more—to suit each mood, and make for a good evening's entertainment. With their exceptional insight and the uncanny ability to disturb and bewitch, these writers will give readers great pleasure, countless frights, and many choice delights.

Helen Hoke

▪William F. Nolan

Dead Call

A telephone call from a dead man can be rather unnerving—especially when he explains that he is "not really using a phone," he's just aligning his "cosmic vibrations to match the vibrations of this power line." Should you listen to the message?

LEN HAD BEEN DEAD for a month when the phone rang.

Midnight. Cold in the house and me dragged up from sleep to answer the call. Helen gone for the weekend. Me, alone in the house. And the phone ringing...

"Hello."

"Hello, Frank."

"Who is this?"

"You know *me*. It's Len...old Len Stiles."

Cold. Deep and intense. The receiver dead-cold metal in my hand.

11

"Leonard Stiles died four weeks ago."

"Four weeks, three days, two hours and twenty-seven minutes ago—to be exact."

"I want to know who *you* are!"

A chuckle. The same dry chuckle I'd heard so many times. "C'mon, old buddy—after twenty years. Hell, you *know* me."

"This is a damned poor joke!"

"No joke, Frank. You're there, alive. And I'm here, dead. And you know something, old buddy? I'm really *glad* I did it."

"Did...what?"

"Killed myself. Because...death is just what I hoped it would be: beautiful...gray...quiet. No pressures."

"Len Stile's death was an accident...a concrete freeway barrier....His car—"

"I *aimed* my car for that barrier. Pedal to the floor. Doing almost a hundred when I hit....No accident, Frank." The voice cold....Cold. "I *wanted* to be dead...and no regrets."

I tried to laugh, make light of this—matching his chuckle with my own. "Dead men don't use telephones."

"I'm not really using a phone, not in a physical sense. It's just that I chose to contact you this way. You might say it's a matter of 'psychic electricity.' As a detached spirit, I'm able to align my cosmic vibrations to match the vibrations of this power line. Simple, really."

"Sure. A snap. Nothing to it."

"Naturally you're skeptical. I expected you to be. But...listen carefully to me, Frank."

And I listened—with the phone gripped in my hand in that cold night house—as the voice told me things that *only* Len could know...intimate details of

12

shared experiences extending back through two decades. And when he'd finished I was certain of one thing:

He *was* Len Stiles.

"But how...I still don't..."

"Think of this phone as a medium—a line of force through which I can bridge the gap between us." The dry chuckle again. "Hell, you gotta admit it beats holding hands around a table in the dark—yet the principle is the same."

I'd been standing by my desk, transfixed by the voice. Now I moved behind the desk, sat down, trying to absorb this dark miracle. My muscles were wire-taut, my fingers cramped about the metal receiver. I dragged in a slow breath, the night dampness of the room pressing at me. "All right...I don't believe in ghosts, don't pretend to understand any of this, but...I'll accept it. I *must* accept it."

"I'm glad, Frank—because it's important that we talk." A long moment of hesitation. Then the voice, lower now, softer. "I *know* how lousy things have been, old buddy."

"What do you mean?"

"I just know how things are going for you. And...I want to help. As your friend, I want you to know that I understand."

"Well...I'm really not—"

"You've been feeling bad, haven't you? Kind of *down*...right?"

"Yeah. A little, I guess."

"And I don't blame you. You've got reasons. Lots of reasons....For one, there's your money problem."

"I'm expecting a raise. Cooney promised me one—within the next few weeks."

"You won't get it, Frank. I *know*. He's lying to you. Right now, at this moment, he's looking for a man to

13

replace you at the company. Cooney's planning to fire you."

"He never liked me. We never got along from the day I walked into that office."

"And your wife...All the arguments you've been having with her lately...It's a pattern, Frank. Your marriage is all over. Helen's going to ask you for a divorce. She's in love with another man."

"*Who,* dammit? What's his name?"

"You don't know him. Wouldn't change things if you did. There's nothing you can do about it now. Helen just...doesn't love you any more. These things happen to people."

"We've been drifting apart for the last year....But I didn't know why. I had no idea that she—"

"And then there's Jan. She's back on it, Frank. Only it's worse now. A lot worse."

I knew what he meant—and the coldness raked along my body. Jan was nineteen, my oldest daughter, and she'd been into drugs for the past three years. But she'd promised to quit.

"What do you know about Jan? Tell me!"

"She's into the heavy stuff, Frank. She's hooked bad. It's too late for her."

"What the hell are you saying?"

"I'm saying she's lost to you....She's rejected you, and there's no reaching her. She *hates* you....Blames you for everything."

"I won't *accept* that kind of blame! I did my best for her."

"It wasn't enough, Frank. We both know that. You'll never see Jan again."

The blackness was welling within me, a choking wave through my body.

"Listen to me, old buddy....Things are going to get worse, not better. I know. I went through my own

14

kind of hell when I was alive."

"I'll...start over. Leave the city. Go east, work with my brother in New York."

"Your brother doesn't want you in his life. You'd be an intruder...an alien. He never writes to you, does he?"

"No, but that doesn't mean—"

"Not even a card last Christmas. No letters or calls. He doesn't *want* you with him, Frank, believe me."

And then he began to tell me other things. He began to talk about middle age, and how it was too late to make any kind of new beginning. He spoke of disease...loneliness...of rejection and despair. And the blackness was complete.

"There's only one real solution to things, Frank— just *one*. That gun you keep in your desk upstairs. *Use* it, Frank. Use the gun."

"I couldn't do that."

"But why not? What other choice have you got? The solution is *there*. Go upstairs and use the gun. I'll be waiting for you afterwards. You won't be alone. It'll be like the old days....We'll be together....Death is beautiful....Use the gun, Frank....The gun....Use the gun. . . . The gun . . . The gun . . ."

I've been dead for a month now, and Len was right. It's fine here. No pressures. No worries. Gray and quiet and beautiful....

I know how lousy things have been going for you. And they won't get any better.

Isn't that your phone ringing?

Better answer it.

It's important that we talk.

▪Nancy C. Swoboda

Christopher Frame

Who has not wished to visit briefly the serenity of a quieter time? To suffuse his present life with the gentleness of a memory? Times past are like a painting, where the harsh outlines of reality are blurred and only the essence of the subject remains. Once or twice in the long night of the soul's darkness, it is possible to transcend the present for a visit to that painting, the home of the soul's gratification.

CHRISTOPHER FRAME looked out the window of his little shop at the rain. It was just after five in the evening and people with umbrellas and colorful raincoats hurried to get home from work. That's all they ever did anymore, he thought. They hurried through their jobs and they hurried through life, and there was no time for pride left in either one. He stirred up the gray lumps of coal in the tiny fireplace

17

until they glowed orangy-red against the blackened grate and returned to his work at the big desk.

The building was incongruous on the modern downtown street. It was two stories high, not too wide, and was sandwiched in between two impersonal-looking steel-and-glass structures. Across the top of the door and big window on either side was an old-fashioned sign in raised brass letters. All it said was FRAMES. For over eighty-two years his father and then Christopher Frame had been in the business of photography—mostly restoration, tinting and oils, and framing. The coincidence of the name had made a descriptive trademark for their work.

Now Christopher was alone at both his job and his life. He lived in the back rooms of the old building and used the barny upstairs for storage and supplies. The ancient brownstone structure had been his home, his world for thirty years. At fifteen he had become his father's apprentice, the same year his mother died, and the two Frames had moved to their place of work to live. When Christopher was thirty his father died, leaving him sole owner of an expensive piece of real estate upon which rested the sum total of his existence.

The rain had settled into a steady drizzle and the gray afternoon was fast darkening into evening. Christopher made himself some tea and toast and studied the picture before him on the desk. He had been looking at it, pondering over it ever since that Mr. Walters had brought it in four days ago. It was a very old photograph of a family outing—on a picnic, probably, but it was badly faded and dog-eared. Mr. Walters wanted it restored and done in oils as a present for his wife. It seemed the picture was of her side of the family and she was very sentimental about such things. Naturally, he entrusted

18

Christopher Frame to do an excellent job. He had even selected a beautiful old gold-leaf frame to finish it off.

And finish it off, Christopher could not do. Briefly, Mr. Walters had mentioned his wife had blue eyes and that her hair was fair when she was a child. But the rest of the people—what of them? Eyes? Hair? What color were their clothes? How blue was the sky? In the background he could make out what looked like a lovely little town with a church spire spearing the clear day, but it was faded, and the family group in the foreground posing on the hillock blurred into various degrees of white outlined and accented in brown.

Pride and perfection went into each piece of his work, and now that picture restoration was so popular it bothered Christopher not to be able to reproduce the photographs faithfully. Most of them were in brown or sepia and the people who brought them in had no idea, of course, of any coloring, since they had been either too young or not even born. He enjoyed creating oil tones for his subjects, but he felt he was misrepresenting the true past somehow. How few craftsmen were left. No one took time anymore— or cared. It was like the difference between some of the beautiful old gold-leaf and hand-carved frames he had stored upstairs and the impersonal and un- interesting modern frames he shuddered to use on his work.

He stirred up the fire and added a bit of coal and then went to the big high-ceilinged room at the back of the shop. It was furnished as a bedroom in massive old mahogany pieces and a big four poster with a patchwork quilt. It was a man's room, but it was warm and cheery—old fashioned. He had the picture with him. He propped it up on the dresser opposite the foot of the bed and then settled himself on top of the quilt for a nap. The timer he used for developing was on the nightstand close by. He set it for one hour and then lay back to contemplate the troublesome photograph. If only he could be there...just long enough to see the true picture, the colors. What a wonderful thing it would be. He dozed off to the measured ticking of the timer.

The combination of something prickling in his ear and an awareness of a bright light brought him back from a heavy sleep to a groggy consciousness. He opened his eyes and looked straight into a stand of lush green grass and above it a horizon of china-blue sky. He was lying on his side under a tree, and it was a beautiful warm sunshiny day!

Cautiously, he rolled over and sat up. The air smelled of sweet clover and the sound of a steeple bell floated lazily in the soft summer breeze. He was on a hill overlooking a neat whitewashed village that nestled against a patchwork quilt of farm land and green slopes. He sat in sheer ecstasy sniffing the clear heady air, but laughter and voices startled him back to the realization that he was in a strange place and an even stranger situation.

Slowly Christopher Frame stood up and peered around the tree. His mouth fell open and a look of shocked disbelief washed over his face. In front of him, living, breathing and posing was the fleshly counterpart of the picture on his dresser! The photographer, his back to Christopher, was placing his subjects and instructing them to stand very still for the camera. The colors were so vivid in the summer sunshine! Christopher stared at the group and memorized as much as he could and then made notes in the little book he always carried. Surely he was dreaming, but perhaps it was some sort of telepathy coming to him from the picture caused by his anxiety to know more about the faded print.

Just as the little girl in the group spied him a loud ticking started in his head and exploded into ringing bells. The picture before him blacked out, and when he could see again he was looking at the ceiling of his own room and the timer had gone off. He sat up on the edge of the bed and glanced at the picture. What a realistic dream, he thought, chuckled and patted the small notebook in his breast pocket. He decided to get to work on the reproduction while the scene was still clear in his mind. If not accurate in detail, at least this work would be inspired.

He stood, stretched, and then on an impulse, reached for the little book. It was warm from being so close to his body. He opened it and drew in his breath. On the page in his neat script was a detailed description of the photograph. In his excitement the book dropped from his trembling hands to the floor. As he stooped to pick it up he saw the green blades of grass caught in the heels of his shoes. Dizzy, with a feeling of strange elation, he sat down again on the bed. Gingerly, he picked up the timer and examined it. It was the same one he had used for years. There was nothing unusual about it now. He put it back on the nightstand and for a long moment stared at the single dial that stared back at him like a benign Cyclops.

The import of his experience left Christopher confused. He hovered between reality and whatever level of consciousness it was where he had been. Slowly he moved from his bedroom to the outer regions of the old building. The coals were now gray ashes in the grate and the rain had stopped. Nothing was different about the familiar surroundings. He opened the front door and took a breath of the cool rain-washed air. Everything outside was the same, too. He liked his street best at night. The electric signs winked against the steel-and-glass buildings and made the cold impersonal structures appear cheery and friendly.

So often it seemed to him that this place was a fortress from within whose walls he could look out and see lovely old stone shops razed and new modern steel-and-concrete monsters thrown up, people hurrying faster each day to skim over their work and hurry home to start all over again. In a way Frames was a monument to the past and he intended that his work would continue in the fine tradition of his heritage.

Many nights as they warmed their feet by the small fireplace Christopher's father had told of the days when it took weeks to turn out one piece of furniture and how most things you bought lasted a lifetime, how men were craftsmen and artisans instead of hurried workers. The pictures, the very old ones that people brought in, made those days seem even more real and desirable to Christopher. After his father died he gathered the walls around him even more closely and worked hard at his profession. He longed for the companionship of a wife, but he was too old-fashioned to be attractive to women, or so he thought. He made himself content in his work and the security of the old building.

The air helped clear his head and he felt free of the lingering cobwebs of his dream. But *was* it a dream? Blades of grass and a detailed description written in his notebook were tangible facts. Anxious to translate all he had "seen" into the photograph, he put aside any further speculation and set to work.

The sun was casting a rosy glow on the pale-gray building across the street when he finished. It was

22

like looking through the gold-leaf frame into the real scene. The vividness with which he had reproduced the picture astounded him. He gazed at the distant church spire and the little village barely visible beyond the smiling group and he felt a faint nostalgic longing. Excitement overcame the melancholy and he lifted the receiver to call Mr. Walters to tell him the picture was finished. Then he realized it was only dawn—much too early. He decided to lie down for a short nap, and after affixing his trademark to the back of the picture he went to his bedroom. With a moment's hesitation he set the old brass alarm clock instead of the timer.

The day was uneventful. Mr. Walters was pleased with the restoration and framing of the photograph, but not overly impressed. Of course, he wasn't aware of Christopher's strange experience. There was a steady stream of customers, but he didn't handle them in his usual meticulous manner. His mind was preoccupied with other thoughts. He kept going over what had happened to him. It had to be real. There was no grass for miles around, and one didn't write as clearly or as coherently in one's sleep as he had done in his little notebook. He knew he would try to make it happen again—now, after closing, and he knew just the picture he would use.

It seemed an eternity until five o'clock. He locked the front door and paused to watch the hurrying parade of people running for buses, rushing to parking lots, all fleeing from work after skimming through the day. Well, he had done the same thing today, too, but this was an exception. It threatened rain again. Christopher started a small fire in the grate, turned off all but the desk lamp and hurried to his bedroom.

Propped up on the dresser, just as he had done with

23

the first one, was another old photograph. It was of a group of young men posing on a wooden sidewalk in front of a glass-fronted store. How many times Christopher's father had told him about all of those eager young fellows and the fine times they had. They, his father included, were all apprentices at various shops, learning a trade for board and room, and sometimes a little extra if they worked especially hard.

Cautiously, he set the timer for one hour and lay down on the bed. Perhaps he would wake up in the town square opposite the store. How strange it would be to see his father as a very young man. In spite of his excitement he did fall asleep, but when the timer rang he was still in his own room and with no knowledge of having been anywhere at all. The picture remained inviolate on the dresser. Disappointment and doubt sapped the benefit of any rest he gained from the short nap.

He sat up most of the night brooding in front of the fire. Why hadn't it worked? The circumstances were almost the same. Maybe it had to be a past of which he had no cognizance. The desire to go back—even more, to prove or disprove the reality of so doing—overwhelmed him. He looked at his pocket watch. There was still time before dawn, and he was a bit sleepy. Carefully he sorted through the file of old photographs waiting to be restored and chose one brought in by a Mrs. Nellie Hampton. He knew nothing of or about her other than that she was a customer.

Again, he placed the picture on the dresser and set the timer at one hour. He studied the faded old print from his bed. It was evidently a party in someone's backyard. There were Japanese lanterns criss-crossed from the porch to the trees, long tables of food, and a

24

smiling group in their best dress standing stiffly on the porch steps. But wait! He jumped up and examined the picture more carefully. There must be something that he could bring back with him—proof of his actually having been there. Ah! That was it. The porch railing had gingerbread spindles topped off by little round wooden balls. He could snap off one of those easily. Quickly he lay back on the bed and after a final look at the picture he closed his eyes.

It was the swaying motion that awakened him—along with the discomfort of the wooden slats in the swing. He was on the porch facing the side yard away from the party in a big chair swing suspended from the ceiling by two stout chains. In front of him, plain as day, was a railing made of ornate spindles topped with little round wooden balls! He stood up and walked slowly to the corner of the porch and peered around the side of the house. As before, the group in the picture posed, waited for the photographer to dismiss them and then moved from the steps back to the festivities.

He was there! He looked at himself. In pants and shirt sleeves he was not too conspicuous, for several of the men had taken off their coats and were pitching horseshoes. He walked nonchalantly down the steps and stayed close to the bushes where he could watch this wonderful old-time party. He was tempted to sample the food. The smells that wafted over to his nose in the balmy air made his mouth water. There were chicken and pie and home-baked rolls and a small crock of freshly churned butter. To the side was a tubful of ice surrounding a big gallon tin of fresh-strawberry ice cream.

"Hello. Would you like something to eat?" The soft voice startled him.

Christopher Frame whirled around and looked into

25

the bluest eyes and sweetest face he had ever seen.

"Wha—? Oh, thank you. No, I've—I've already eaten."

"You're new, aren't you? My name is Sarah Phillips."

She looked at him with such genuine interest that on top of the headiness of being here he felt a strange new sort of dizzying elation.

"Er, yes. I've just arrived in time for the party."

"I'm glad you could come, Mr.—— Oh, I'm sorry. I didn't catch your name."

"Christopher...Christopher Frame."

"What part of the country are you from?"

Although she still regarded him with interest, he could see that she was curious about his appearance.

"I—I'm a photographer. I travel a lot."

"Will you be here long?" Her golden curls shone in the sun.

"I don't think so. I'm not sure."

He looked at her hard and tried to fix a picture of her in his mind. Then the loud ticking started in his head.

"Mr. Frame? Are you all right?"

"Yes, but you must excuse me. I want very much to stay, but I must go now."

"I'm sorry you have to leave. I hope we'll meet again." A tiny frown crossed her brow.

"And so do I, Miss Phillips...Sarah. Good-bye."

The ticking was deafening now. He had to hurry. He walked rapidly out of sight around the side of the house. He barely managed to snap off a little wooden ball from the railing before the bell rang.

He was lying on his back when he awoke. The first rays of sun shone through the window to cast a pinkish hue on the ceiling. He was afraid to move, afraid to leave behind the last wisp of the world he had found but could not hold on to. Then he remembered the railing. Perhaps he did hang on. Slowly he closed both hands. Nothing. Despair engulfed him, not only for losing the past, but for losing Sarah Phillips.

He had been the victim of his own vivid dreams—dreams that had opened the floodgates to yearnings he had kept quietly within himself for so long.

He stood up and walked over to the picture. She was there, smiling out at him, but the faded print obscured her simple beauty. How foolish, he thought, to fall in love with the past and then with a girl who was part of it. Well, at least Mrs. Nellie Hampton would have an imaginative restoration when he finished. With a sigh he started for the front of the building. Getting to work would help a little. He stopped and looked at the timer. Perhaps he should get a new one. Then he glanced at the bed, looked again and cried aloud. Hidden by the busy pattern of the patchwork quilt was a little round wooden ball!

Clutching the picture and the precious little piece of the past, a euphoric Christopher Frame staggered out to his desk and sat down heavily. It was all true. He had actually gone back into time prescribed by the old photos. Then a terrible thought crossed his mind. Just how long would he be able to go back? What if the timer broke? Tenderly he put the picture back on his desk and turned on the bright light. He studied Sarah's dear face through a magnifying glass, and suddenly he knew what he would do.

All day he worked hard to complete as much as he could. Pride and integrity still governed his actions despite the wild thoughts that whirled in his head. Anyway, he wanted to be good and tired by nightfall. As was his custom, he closed for an hour at lunchtime. He went to the second floor. Everything was neat, cataloged and in order. He browsed through the small storeroom, where all of the old family heirlooms were kept. Admiringly he ran his hands over the carving in the high-backed chair, held a cranberry glass goblet up to the light, studied the inlaid mother-of-pearl design in the graceful little secretary. Today any of these objects would be priced beyond the average person's reach. In the past such fine things were commonly available. It made him tingle to think of working among such artisans as those who considered doing no less than their best in every detail.

By closing time he was satisfied with his accomplishments and he was really very tired. He looked out the front window as if he hoped to see something other than the usual five-o'clock rush, shrugged and turned away. Carefully he took the picture from his desk, glanced around once more and went to his bedroom. It was almost like a ritual now. Again he placed the old photograph on the dresser— just as it had been the night before. Sarah was still there, smiling out from the past.

Beyond the picture he could see himself in the dresser mirror. His hair was rumpled and his shirt was flecked with oil paint and developing chemicals. Quickly, for he felt a great weariness overtaking him, he put on a fresh shirt and combed his hair. Then, with trembling hands, he set the timer for one hour. He was tempted to set it for a longer period, but he was afraid to upset the pattern. With a nervous little sigh he stretched out on the bed and shut his eyes tightly.

From far away he could hear her calling, and then closer—almost in his ear. He felt his head cradled in something soft and crinkly. Slowly, he opened his eyes and gazed into the face of a very worried-looking

Sarah Phillips. She was holding his head in her lap.

"Christopher! Mr. Frame? Are you all right?"

"Sarah!" He started to get up.

"Now, just be still for a bit. You didn't look well when you rushed off around the side of the house. That's where I found you."

"Found me?"

"Yes."

"I—I guess I must have let the heat get to me."

"Do you feel able to get up now? I can get you a glass of cool lemonade."

"No, I'm fine." Regretfully, he left the haven of her lap and stood up. "I'd feel better if we could walk a little."

He had to know if the realm of the past extended beyond the house, the backyard party, the smiling group on the porch steps. He offered Sarah his arm and she took it with a shy, pleased smile.

They walked out to the front of the house. It was all there—the tree-lined street, the big whitewashed homes. They strolled slowly, deliciously, and he couldn't begin to absorb the richness of the surroundings. Two blocks over, they came to the town square, lushly green and manicured, surrounded by charming little shops in stone and wood buildings. This was where he wanted to be. Oh, if only...then he heard the ticking start.

"Sarah, I've decided to settle here. Would—would that please you? I mean, well..."

"Yes, Christopher, it would. I'm very glad...but you have that strange look again. Perhaps we've walked too much."

"Perhaps we have. Let's go back to the party. But, Sarah? Just for a time, hold my hand—and don't let go for anything."

She looked frightened and the ticking in his head

29

was deafening now. He could feel the firm pressure of her soft hand holding his. At last, they reached the house and went around to the back. Just before the bell went off he tightened his grip on Sarah's hand and shut his eyes.

It was three days before anyone called the authorities' attention to Christopher Frame's unannounced absence. Several of his customers with pictures promised them by the faithful Mr. Frame became concerned and two detectives were sent to check up on him. They found nothing amiss in the building, nor did they find any trace of Christopher Frame.

One of the officers discovered the picture on the dresser. "Hey, Charlie. Come in here. Want ya to see this."

"What's up?"

"See this picture? Just so's you'll know who we're looking for. Must be a relative of old Chris's from way back. Sure looks just like him."

"Which one?"

The detective pointed a big finger at the faded print. "Here. This one—holding hands with the girl on the porch."

▪Mary Elizabeth Counselman

The Huaco of Señor Peréz

High in the Peruvian mountains a man meets his destiny when he buys an ancient drinking cup from an old peasant. With the sale of the cup comes an ancient story of torture and death four hundred years old, which returns to haunt the buyer in a most perilous way.

STANDING BESIDE THE ANCIENT FOUNTAIN in the square, letting his shrewd eyes wander over the peaceful scene, Joe Conti thought: Excellent place to find artifacts, relics—antiques to be bought for a song! His alert gaze missed nothing.

Stone-block buildings with red tile roofs huddled close to the narrow streets, where a scattering of Spanish-Indian inhabitants moved with slow deliberation about their morning tasks. Beyond the town, one could see little terraced farms clinging to this bleak slope of the Andes, with here and there a

31

herd of llamas or alpacas like long-necked sheep. Those low, thatch-roofed stone huts had housed these highlanders for centuries—cold, cramped abodes with no more modern conveniences than their grandsires had possessed.

There was a timeless quality about the scene that vaguely disturbed Conti. That temple-to-the sun, for instance—those mortarless granite blocks must have been put together by manpower as early as 1200 A.D. Wind-gnawed, sun-bleached, crumbling before the onslaughts of time and weather, the old ruins yet seemed to defy destruction. Even the smells—damp wool, bird guano, quinoa grain—had probably changed little since the time of Francisco Pizarro!

Conti had a perverse desire to toss a grenade into the center of that temple courtyard, if only to see these stolid Peruvians jolted out of their granite serenity. Contentment irritated him. How could one make a sharp trade with a man who desired nothing more than this?

A thin piping caught his ear above the murmur in the square. As he glanced toward the sound, an old *mestizo* came trudging along the worn street, playing a folktune on his *queña* and driving before him two bony, over-burdened llamas. The pack animals veered to drink at the fountain, and the Spanish-Indian followed suit, sweeping off his round-crowned, broad-brimmed hat to splash water over his white hair.

The rising sun was beginning to beat down with a vengeance. He grinned at Conti wilting in his immaculate gray flannels and gasping a bit from *soroche,* the altitude sickness that always affected foreign visitors at more than thirteen thousand feet above sea level.

"Buenos días," Conti greeted, because it was expected.

32

"Ah, Señor tourist! *Buenos días!*" The Peruvian bowed politely. "It is very hot today, no? I, whose family have lived here in Sinchi Rocca for many centuries, even I am melting like the snows on the crest of old Huascarán!"

"Yes. Very hot." Conti suppressed an amused smile at the flowery manner of speech these South Americans used, even for remarks about the weather. Brushing aside further amenities, he came straight to the point of his visit. *"Amigo mio,* do you know where I can buy any—old things? Family heirlooms? I'm Joseph Conti, purchasing agent for the Hanover Museum in New York. Private collection. Not open to the public except for charity exhibits or—"

He broke off, telling himself that this ignorant half-breed would have no idea what he was talking about in his careful textbook Spanish.

But the bright black eyes set high in the narrow swarthy face were regarding him with unusual intelligence.

"Antiques?" The old man nodded knowingly. "Ah, yes. Always the North American tourists wish to buy the mementos of our historic past—for reasons unknown to me! Inca relics? Gold ornaments? Featherwork? Or"— his voice turned faintly harsh and bitter—"perhaps some trifle discarded by the *Conquistadores,* when they came here seeking power over our ancient people. And gold! Always more and more gold!"

He lapsed abruptly into Quichua, the Indian language. Conti caught a few words he knew, and they were certainly not very complimentary to the Spanish invaders. The old *mestizo* spat with such venom that one of his llamas shied nervously.

The North American smiled. "But you are half-Spanish yourself, are you not?" he taunted. "At least

33

one of your Inca ancestors made peace with the *Conquistadors!* No?"

The old man's pleasant expression faded.

"One must live," he murmured in coldly formal Spanish that made Conti abruptly change his tack, with the psychology of the clever trader.

"How true! I, too, am half-Indian," he lied skillfully. "Spanish and Comanche." Actually he was a Sicilian immigrant, but he had long ago learned to identify himself with the ethnic background of a possible sucker. "The Spanish invaders overran our continent also, you know. Greedy for land and gold! In this, we are brothers, Señor...?"

"Peréz. Juan Proaña Cusi y Peréz. Your servant!"

The old man, ludicrously shabby in his peasant garb, made a low bow, and rewarded Conti with a smile of total acceptance. He knelt beside his llamas to adjust the woven straps that held their baskets of vicuña wool in place.

Then, bending over the fountain, he thrust a native drinking bottle under the thin trickle, piped long ago from some icy spring far up the mountainside. Patiently he held the double-flask until one of them brimmed over. Conti watched idly—

And then, suddenly, he came to a point like a birddog scenting game.

The bottle was handsomely cast of bronze, its dual flagons jointed at neck and bottom by two thin pipes that allowed their contents to flow from one to the other. Each flask was molded in the likeness of an Inca face—one calmly smiling, the other scowling in fierce anger, much like the two masks of Comedy and Tragedy in Greek drama. The mouths of the flasks, corked with ornate metalwork, sprouted up from each head like a feather headdress. In the center of each

34

forehead was a medallion in the likeness of the rising sun.

Conti ran his tongue over dry lips. The bottle was pre-Columbian, and therefore very valuable. The workmanship was early Inca, perhaps 1000 A.D. if he had learned anything while working as a guide for the Metropolitan. The molded hair was long and straight in the Indian style, the slightly almond-shaped eyes set high in the long-nosed, large-eared faces. Not peasant faces, but those of the *Orejones*— Great Ears; the Inca nobility.

Conti leaned closer. On the thin bronze pipe that joined the two bottlenecks there was some sort of inscription—not Inca, certainly, since they had no written language of any kind. He tried to make out the words, worn almost away by years of handling.

"What does it say there?" he asked casually as the *mestizo* glanced up and noted his interest. "That drinking bottle...it looks as though it might be a *huaco*—a holy object found in some Inca tomb. But the inscription! Spanish words on an Inca replica? Er...may I...?"

With native courtesy the Peruvian handed him the half-filled bottle.

"Sí," he nodded reverently. "It is indeed a *huaco,* señor—our Quichua word, spelled many ways by the Spanish. It once belonged to an ancestor of mine. The Inca—the word originally meant *ruler*—of this village, in fact. A cousin of the Great One, Atahualpa—descendant of all the great Incas as far back as Manco Capac, he who led our people out of the south into the rising sun..."

"Yes, yes, of course..."

Conti was peering at the inscription, trying hard to hide the glint of cupidity in his eyes.

35

"Bébaselo con inocencia," he read with difficulty, then translated: *"Drink up...with...innocence?* Of what, Señor Perez?" He laughed. "The misery of *la perseguidora*—hangover? This *is* a drinking bottle, is it not? Used at banquets?" He winked broadly. "I've heard your Inca grandees really lived it up! Carousing and making love to the Chosen Ones, the temple virgins. Some of those figures on Inca pottery are so frank, they can't be exhibited to the public!...Servant!" he called in mocking mimicry. "More *chicha*— at once!"

Rakishly he placed the mouth of the empty flask to his lips and blew into it, to make the whistling sound with which Inca revelers once signaled for a refill of the strong native beer brewed from sprouted maize. The old *mestizo* nodded, with a slight smile acknowledging the foreigner's uncommon erudition about Peruvian customs. But his eyes registered disapproval of Conti's flippant manner.

"En verdad! Just so did my ancestors call for more wine at feasts. But the Old Ones were beyond sin, señor." His tone of reproof matched his eyes. "They were gods—children of the Sun, our ancient deity...."

He took back the *huaco* gently but firmly, as one might remove a crucifix from profane hands.

"But the inscription?" Conti insisted. "Isn't it a kind of toast? An invitation to drink and be merry, with no...qualms of conscience?"

"Perhaps it has a deeper meaning," the Peruvian suggested humbly. "I am not a man of letters, but...perhaps it means: *Drink with...an innocent heart?* Innocent of treachery, of greed?"

The purchasing agent squirmed, eyeing him narrowly. But there was no hidden look of accusation in the stolid half-Indian face.

"With an innocent heart, eh? Peace, goodwill toward men...?"

"*Sí!*" The old man nodded, with the quick smile of a child. "As Christians take Communion. Even as the Disciples drank wine together at the Last Supper—so drank the ancient ones of my people as they dined together in harmony. Besides," his voice sank to a near-whisper, "that meaning would bear out the...the legend!"

"Legend?" Conti stiffened. "There's some sort of legend connected with your *huaco* there?"

He lowered his gaze to the bottle in the *mestizo*'s hand as he held the empty flask at the fountain to fill it also. Like any experienced dealer in antiques, the agent knew well how a story attached to some relic could zoom its value to buyers. Even an undocumented story—since one could always forge proof by some obscure authority.

"Not a story recorded in writing by the Spanish," the old man deprecated. "Only by word of mouth among my people, the Quichua. The bottle is cursed, señor! For this reason I have not given it to the museum at Sucré, where other such *huacos* are kept safe from..."

"Oh, I see!" Conti peered at him sharply. Perhaps the old half-breed was not as naive as he seemed! Was this only a clever pitch to raise the price? But, again, as he looked into the direct dark eyes, he saw no trace of the hidden deception in his own.

"It is dangerous," the Peruvian explained. "Many have died because of its power. Many! This is why I cannot bring myself to sell it. Only a simple man, like myself, could use it, drink from it daily, without...consequences."

"Consequences?" The purchasing agent struggled

to make his tone casual. "What sort of—?"

"Death, señor! Death by thirst, a slow and painful one! As I said, the bottle once belonged to my ancestor, Titu Cusi, Inca of this village in the time of Atahualpa. He whom the invaders..."

"Yes, yes; I know about Atahualpa," Conti cut him short, unable to curb his impatience. "How Pizarro captured him at Cuzco, and imprisoned him in a room about fifteen feet square. How he promised to fill that room with gold, if they would release him. Gold to the height of a man's head—imagine!" The agent's eyes glittered. "Literally a king's ransom!"

"*Correcto!* And he paid that ransom, as promised! But—" The old man's face went hard as the crumbling granite wall behind him. "Pizarro killed him anyway! *El alevoso*—the treacherous one! He feared Atahualpa's power! And even a roomful of gold was not enough for those greedy ones. After his murder, the *Conquistadores* came even to this village, seeking the source of the gold! My ancestor had sent seven llamas loaded with it, to help raise the ransom. They captured him, our Titu Cusi, and staked him out on the mountainside..."

"No!" Conti pretended shocked sympathy. "They tortured him?"

"*Sí!*" The *mestizo*'s voice was a harsh whisper, like the sound of a chill wind blowing down the narrow street. "They tortured him, señor, beyond belief! First, they fed him oversalted meat. Then, they...they staked him out, face up to the blazing sun! His eyelid muscles were cut, you understand, so that he could not close his eyes; could not even blink. He lay thus for endless days of thirst and heat. It shriveled his skin! Blackened his parched tongue! Baked his eyeballs until they were as rotten grapes! At last thirst closed his throat, like a hand...choking...!"

38

The dark eyes narrowed with hate. "A refinement of cruelty that only the Spanish could have conceived, señor—to torture an Inca with *sunlight!*"

Involuntarily Conti gulped, his own throat gone dry. He tried to shake off the spell of the old man's story. But the harsh whisper went on and on:

"*Sí*, señor! And above Cusi's head they tied his drinking-bottle, this *huaco,* so that its contents dripped out, inches from his parched lips! Drop by drop...driving him mad with thirst! When it hung empty, the soldiers blew into it to make it whistle for a refill—as you yourself did just now, with unintended sacrilege. Mocking our ancient custom! For it is actually a prayer to the Sun, our deity, a plea to fill our need, whatever it may be. Warmth. Food. Or, in the case of my brave ancestor, only a swallow of water! Or—merciful death!"

"But the inscription?" Conti reminded. "You haven't..."

"Ah!" The old man nodded. "It was then that it appeared on that metal pipe. A warning! In Spanish, so that the greedy ones might have their last fair chance to...No one knows who inscribed it there. Perhaps the spirit of Atahualpa? Perhaps even great Manco Capac himself! Or—?" The *mestizo* smiled blandly. "Perhaps there is no inscription, but only some corrosion on the bronze...? *Es posible.* The words are faint.

"For seven days they tortured my ancestor. But Cusi would not tell the secret of our village gold! Alas for our people, it died with him, there on that mountainside. Then they came to bury him, breaking pottery and killing many beasts and tearing much woven cloth—a funeral custom of the Quichua, señor, so that the dead may carry their possessions with them to the spirit world....They were about to smash this bottle, too, for his use. But a soldier named Peréz"—the old man spat out the name like a bad taste, "took a fancy to it. He stole it—along with my ancestor's young daughter, a temple virgin! He took them, and drained them both, and tossed them aside, that evil one, when he had had his fill!"

"*El Perro*—the dog!" Conti murmured. But his lips twitched with covert amusement at this old fool's vehemence about something that had happened so long ago. "So he was the *Conquistador* who . . . ?"

"A conquered people," the *mestizo* nodded bitterly, "must bear the features of the conqueror, along with his yoke! But, he was punished, that one!" The Indian eyes gleamed with triumph. "Oh, yes! He died even as my ancestor died—screaming in a delirium of thirst! Begging for a drink!"

Conti grinned openly. "An alcoholic, was he? Yes, I don't suppose the Spanish could handle your native *chicha!*" he agreed lightly. "Ah well, it served him right. A wonderful tale of poetic justice," he murmured, casually fingering the *huaco* hanging now from the llama's pack. "A very interesting relic. My directors might be persuaded to pay you—" The agent moved in smoothly:"Say, fifty *sols* for it?"

"Oh no." The Peruvian smiled politely, but shook his head. "I dare not, señor! What if others like that Spanish soldier should drink from it, without heeding the inscription? Many have done so...and died as he died! And who, in these days of avarice and deception, can truly be said to have an innocent heart? A heart like those of...the Children of the Sun?"

Once more Conti threw him a sharp look, trying to read that stolid Indian face. But there seemed to be no double meaning to the old man's words. What

40

nonsense! Though the Peruvian obviously believed it. If he was to obtain that valuable relic—

"You are right!" the purchasing agent agreed skillfully. "The curse is dangerous! Therefore—would it not be safer, Señor Peréz, for this *huaco* to be placed in a sealed showcase? In a museum, where no one at all would ever drink from it again? With, beside it," Conti pursued, "a printed account of the legend, so that all men may learn the wisdom of your ancient people? What a gift to the modern world!" he gestured dramatically. "And what a fitting tribute to your unfortunate ancestor—the Inca, Cusi, who died a noble death...!"

He kept his gaze on the *huaco,* watching Peréz from the corner of his hard eyes. Conti's lips twitched as he saw the shabby old half-breed draw himself up with a lost pride. His stolid face was alight with something that poverty and toil had all but worn away, like the altar stone of the temple ruins behind him.

"Did I say fifty *sols?*" Conti murmured. "Perhaps my directors would make it a hundred. Not for the value of the *huaco,*" he shrugged, "for it has none. An old bottle? But—as a gesture of goodwill, señor, from my America to yours? The money, of course, will be put in your trust. For those of your village who may be in need of...oh, some little *bonita* such as your ancestor might bestow on the poor." Conti pretended not to notice the old man's worn poncho, his ragged blue pants, his bare feet. "An extra ration of *chicha?* Or...*coca?*"

The native beamed, drawing himself up still further with a pathetic dignity.

"Coca?"

For the first time Conti noticed an old Quichua

41

woman, hovering in the background with a stairstep flock of children. She edged forward—evidently the old man's wife. Her calloused fingers still moved, ceaselessly spinning alpaca wool in the old way on two rough spindles. One of the thin children was fondling a *cuy,* the domesticated rat of the Indians, raised as pets—and, eventually, food. The boy spoke eagerly, but the old woman silenced him with a gesture. Conti noted the avid way she was clutching a small bag of the narcotic leaves, chewed by the Indians as their only bulwark against disease and exhaustion and the rigors of their daily life.

"Coca—sí, mucha coca!" the agent promised enticingly.

To clinch the sale, he pulled from his pockets all the small change and American bills he had on him—about fourteen dollars. With a flourish he tossed it into one of the pack-baskets of vicuña wool, cannily aware of how little cash this poverty-stricken family must have seen in their entire lifetime.

The old man gasped. His wife crowded closer, the children clustering about them with excited questions about the money.

"Madre de Dios!" The *mestizo* touched it with one finger, fumbling for his quipu, that small cluster of colored strings with which the natives keep accounts. "How many *sols* is that? Fifty?"

"Enough to serve you until I can send more," Conti evaded. "Well? A bargain?"

He reached out gently, with a great show of reverence, and untied the *huaco* from the pack animal. The old man lifted his hand, hesitant, then shrugged and let it fall.

"So be it," he murmured. "For the honor of my ancestor. And the welfare of our village poor!"

He was trying to count the money, waving back his

42

eager family with stern gestures. Conti tucked the drinking-bottle under his coat, and bowed farewell before the Peruvian could change his mind.

"*Vaya con Dios,* Señor Peréz! I will guard your *huaco* with my life!"

"*Con Dios...*"

The purchasing agent moved away quickly. Dazzled by the sight of the cash, the Indian had not even asked him for a receipt with statement of balance due!

Then—Conti's eyes narrowed suddenly. In that case, why should he turn over the costly relic to the Hanover Museum for a mere commission? Why not smuggle it through customs, by methods he had used before, and sell it himself in New York for a small fortune? Conti grinned as he ducked into the doorway of a nearby *tambo.* What collector would not pay well for such a find? And then? Wine and women for Joe Conti, he exulted, the like of which no Inca had ever enjoyed!

He glanced back at the little group by the fountain, still in an excited huddle, their faces transfigured like those of slum children promised their first Christmas tree. The agent watched them as they moved out of sight down the hilly cobblestone street. The thin piping of the old man's flute drifted back to him—

Or— Was that eerie whistling sound coming from the drinking-bottle hidden under his coat? Conti shook his head sharply; slapped his temple. Confound this rarefied atmosphere! There was a ringing in his ears. The *soroche* made him feel light and queer, strangely nervous and uneasy.

He strode out into the street, headed for the airport. The sooner he got out of South America with this contraband historical relic, the better! Three bronze axes and a *champi*—an Indian crowbar—which he

43

had purchased last week in Cuzco, would satisfy the Hanover board of directors. Once back in New York, he would sell this *huaco,* under the counter, to—Conti grinned. Perhaps he would even sell it back to the Archaeological Museum in Sucré, where it rightfully belonged!

As for sending Señor Peréz the rest of the promised hundred *sols*—Conti laughed shortly. What man needed to remain poor? *Do others before they do you,* was his Golden Rule, since his parents had abandoned him on a church doorstep!

Chuckling, he hurried toward the Sinchi Rocca airport, where a light plane was about to take off for Lima.

A week later he was aboard an airliner out of Rio, headed for New York. The *huaco,* gaudily painted with a removable waterpaint to resemble some cheap souvenir, he carried with him, wrapped in brown paper like a last-minute gift for someone back home. The customs officer waved it by with scarcely a glance—a quarter of a million dollars' worth of pre-Columbian artifact which was not supposed to leave the country.

Vastly pleased with himself, Joe Conti dozed in his plane seat. When a pretty stewardess offered hot coffee, he leered at her with appreciation and shook his head.

"No, thanks, beautiful! I brought my lunch!" He winked and patted the half-wrapped bottle, which passengers often carried aboard filled with rum punch for the journey.

The stewardess raised her brows, and dodged his caressive hand.

It was at that moment that the big plane lurched and slid sidewise. It lost altitude quickly. The warning sign—*Fasten Seat Belts*—flashed on, and the copilot spoke soothingly over the intercom. *There was no real danger, if everyone would keep calm—life jackets under the seats, with instructions for inflating—life rafts to accommodate everyone.*

In twenty minutes, incredulous and badly shaken, Joe Conti found himself huddled in a bouncing rubber raft with nine more of the sunken plane's passengers. His luggage was gone, along with the relics he had purchased in Cuzco. But he was still clutching the *huaco*—its camouflage paint washing off in spots as a breaker rolled over them. Two of the women were sobbing hysterically, and an elderly gentleman was threatening to sue the airline.

As the morning sun rose higher, blue water stretched out around them, melting into the horizon. The sea was calm enough, but the sun beat down, unmercifully hot. By noon the passengers in Conti's raft had drunk up half the emergency water ration. One of the women noticed his drinking bottle, from which he kept taking covert sips. Her whimpering child reached for it, but Conti shrugged and shook his head.

"Rum and cola," he lied quickly.

It was lucky he had forgotten to empty the twin-flasks since buying it from Senor Peréz. The water from that Sinchi Rocca fountain tasted stale and faintly brackish, but it might save his life. And why share it with strangers who meant nothing to him?

The purchasing agent tilted the *huaco* to his lips again. How hot and dry he felt! His mouth seemed to be filled with sand. And his eyes! He found himself staring up at that bronze disk of sun, unable to look away, unable to blink—Conti laughed at himself uneasily. That little horror tale of the old *mestizo*'s had been a trifle too vivid!

By sundown the rescue planes still had not located

45

their position. Night fell like a sooty lid clapped over the caldron of the Atlantic. A few stars twinkled overhead, like holes in the sooty lid, but there was no moon. A wind sprang up, blowing them farther from the crash area. And when morning came, the sun beat down again as though determined to bake them alive.

Thirst was plaguing all those huddled in the raft. But Conti noted with irritation, he himself seemed to be suffering most, despite his covert pulls at the double bottle. By noon he had drained the last drop from both flasks, but his mouth seemed stuffed with cotton. His skin had shriveled. His lips were cracked and swollen. By three o'clock he lay panting in the bottom of the raft, his tongue protruding from his mouth.

"Water!" Conti gasped as a crewman bent over him. "For God's sake, give me—a drink!"

"You should know better than to keep swigging that rum punch!" the man snapped. He took the *huaco* from Conti's limp hand, and sniffed, then tasted the contents. His face changed. "Water? You had more—?" His stern look softened at sight of Conti's tortured face. "What's wrong with you, fella? Some kind of fever? You've had more liquid than any five of us! And yet...you look as if you'd been adrift for two weeks instead of two days! Hangover, maybe?"

"No!" Conti rasped. "I just...need a *drink!* Please! *Please!* These other people can spare..."

By five o'clock he had lapsed into delirium. The frightened women hunched as far from him as they could get, listening to him rave—first in English and Spanish, then in Quichua....He seemed to be cursing that blazing ball of fire overhead, and the next moment praying to it as though it could hear!

46

As dusk fell, the rescue plane located them. Joseph Conti, agent for the Hanover Museum, was the first passenger to be lifted aboard and given aid. The medic took one look at him and frowned in bewilderment.

"One thousand cc's of glucose for this one!" he snapped. "And another thousand of normal saline solution. He may not make it to the hospital! Only two days' exposure? Why, I never saw such a case of dehydration!"

Conti opened his eyes briefly—shriveled, bloodshot orbs that shocked even the medic.

"Water!" he whispered feebly, and lapsed again into delirium.

Distorted shapes moved about him. At first he thought he was lying in a hospital bed, with a worried-looking intern bending over him on one side, an elderly resident doctor on the other. A subdued light shone down from the ceiling—

Then the figures changed. The intern's face took on the thin, cruel features of a Spanish soldier in the ornate armor of Pizarro's men. The resident—a bearded *Conquistador!* There was a pointed stiletto in his hand, flashing in the blazing sun that shone overhead. With its sharp point he jabbed at Conti's upper arm, demanding again and again in an echoing yammer: *"Where is the gold? The gold? The gold? Where...?"*

Conti's vision cleared. The resident stepped back, hypodermic in hand.

"That's his third thousand cc's of glucose," he grunted to the younger intern on Conti's left. "But he's not responding! I don't understand..." He shook the agent gently. "Where did you get the water in that souvenir bottle, man? You may have been poisoned!"

47

"P-poisoned?" Conti rallied briefly to scowl up at them. "Yes! That's it! That damned *mestizo!* He was afraid I'd want my money back, that lousy fourteen dollars I..."

He turned his head weakly on the pillow, nodding toward the *huaco* on the bedside table with his watch and wallet. His bloodshot eyes rolled toward the intern, who caught his meaning. He shrugged.

"Oh yes, of course. We've already analyzed the contents. Nothing! Pure spring water. There may be something in the metal. To test it," he smiled, "we would have to melt it down. Is it worth anything? The way you hung on to it, even half conscious...!"

"*No!* No, no, you—mustn't destroy it! Sentimental value—"

Conti shook his head violently, reaching for his prize. His hand fell limply. He stared at it, stunned by the sight of his desiccated flesh. Like a mummy's hand! Like a sere leaf from which the sap has drained away! His dry tongue clove to the roof of his mouth. The intern bent over him with a glass of water, but Conti could not seem to swallow.

"We've been pouring liquids into you on the half-hour," the resident said grimly. "We've tried everything! What is it, man? Something chronic? Have you ever before...?"

"N-no..."

Conti stared up at him. His eyes wandered from the grave bearded face to the splotchily painted drinking bottle on the table. The smiling features of the left-hand flask were obscured by paint. But the angry one glowered at him accusingly. The almond eyes and sad mouth reminded him of someone. Where had he seen such a face? On a shabby old Peruvian native, driving two overburdened llamas to market for a few soles to feed his half-starved family? The

48

bronze eyes seemed to bore into his fevered brain. The bronze lips whispered something. *"Bébaselo con...!"*

Conti pointed frantically toward his possessions on the table. The intern bent close to catch his faint whisper.

"My wallet! Hundred dollars...inside. Wire at once to..." He whispered a name and the address of a little village high in the Andes. The intern wrote it down, nodding.

"Last request, I suppose," he murmured, aside to the resident. "Poor devil! I guess he knows he's dying...Confound it!" The young man exploded. "Why can't we do something for him?"

The older medic pursed his lips thoughtfully, and picked up the *huaco*. He turned it around and around in his hands.

"Maybe there's some kind of secret compartment for poison. Like those Borgia wine goblets; you know? With a cache inside, to dissolve and poison their enemies at banquets? Or...Maybe the metal is toxic. If he'd only let us test it! Surely, to save his life...!"

He glanced at Conti, who had overheard. The mummy-face on the pillow was contorted with some emotional conflict—greed vying with fear. But there was no kindness, no remorse, no feeling for anyone but himself in Conti's look. He glared up at the two doctors.

"All right!" The purchasing agent nodded weakly. "Melt it down! Test it! But—" His cracked lips curled in a sneer. "Never mind wiring that...that money! The telegram to Sinchi Rocca—cancel it!"

The intern glanced around suddenly. There was a faint, shrill *whistling sound* in the quiet room. It seemed to be coming from that double bottle in the resident's hands, like air escaping from a balloon. Or, no—not coming from it, but entering into it, as if

49

some eerie force of wind were blowing into the uncorked mouth, as hillybilly musicians blow into a jug.

At the sound, Joseph Conti began to choke...

Turning swiftly, the resident strode out into the hospital corridor, heading for the laboratory. He thrust his patient's drinking bottle into the technician's hands.

"Take this thing apart like a dollar watch. Examine every crack! Test the metal for anything toxic. Arsenic; something of the kind. But—make it fast!"

He hurried back to Conti's room, where the intern was inserting a glucose tube in the agent's nose. He was about the inject another normal saline solution into his veins, when Conti sat erect with a strangled cry, clawing at his throat and gagging.

"Water!" he rasped. *"Aqua!"*

His shriveled eyes bulged as he gasped for breath. Frantically he pointed to his wallet on the bedside table; struggled to speak. But only a dry rattle came from his closing throat. He fell back, dead.

Minutes later, as the intern was pulling the sheet up over Conti's face, the lab technician burst into the room. In his hands were twisted bits of bronze that had once been molded into two Inca faces, now quite unrecognizable. He held them out to the resident, who was writing on the chart at the foot of Conti's bed.

"Good thing this wasn't valuable," the technician began. "We tested every square inch of it, just as you...oh!" he broke off and shook his head ruefully. "Too late, huh? Well," he shrugged, "we didn't find a thing, anyhow. Just an old bronze bottle, with a drop or two of water still in that little connecting pipe. I analyzed it. Pure water. With a slight metallic sediment, nontoxic..."

Moving together, the three stared down at Conti's body—more mummylike than ever under the sheet. The resident flipped back a corner of it briefly, frowning at the desiccated face. The mouth, in rigor mortis, had taken on a weirdly ironic grin, as if the dead man had just caught the point of some macabre joke. The resident laid the remnants of the *huaco* on the table beside Conti's wallet.

"Death by...thirst? It's incredible! Didn't the ancient Peruvians bury broken household objects with their dead?" he commented wryly. "Pots, tools, weapons? Our patient will at least have a drinking bottle to take with him—wherever he's going!"

The intern grunted in response to the mirthless jest.

"Strange case, all right," he murmured. "Could his condition have been psychosomatic? He kept muttering something about a...a curse! Every time he lapsed into delirium..."

"Your guess is as good as mine!" the resident admitted. "There was nothing organic to cause a condition like that, absolutely nothing! By the way," he turned to the lab man, "you mentioned some nontoxic sediment in the water. Metallic...?"

"Yes, gold dust," the technician shrugged. "Quite a lot of it! It had settled in that little connecting pipe between the flasks. You say the bottle was filled at a fountain in Sinchi Rocca? Probably flows from a spring high in the mountains above town. Smack through the middle of a gold mine, from the looks of it! If a man were to trace that stream,"—he laughed lightly—"he could make himself as rich as one of those Inca kings!"

51

▪Alexander Woollcott

Moonlight Sonata

A night spent in the eerie surroundings of a sixteenth-century manor house, under the baleful influence of the full moon, is a formidable combination. It is not surprising that the young visitor's bizarre experience was destined to haunt him.

IF THIS REPORT were to be published in its own England, I would have to cross my fingers in a little foreword explaining that all the characters were fictitious—which stern requirement of the British libel law would embarrass me slightly because none of the characters is fictitious, and the story—told to Katharine Cornell by Clemence Dane and by Katharine Cornell told to me—chronicles what, to the best of my knowledge and belief, actually befell a young English physician whom I shall call Alvan Barach, because that does not happen to be his name. It is an account of a hitherto unreported adventure he

53

had two years ago when he went down into Kent to visit an old friend—let us call *him* Ellery Cazalet— who spent most of his days on the links and most of his nights wondering how he would ever pay the death duties on the collapsing family manor-house to which he had indignantly fallen heir.

This house was a shabby little cousin to Compton Wynyates, with roof-tiles of Tudor red making it cozy in the noonday sun, and a hoarse bell which, from the clock tower, had been contemptuously scattering the hours like coins ever since Henry VIII was a rosy stripling. Within, Cazalet could afford only a doddering couple to fend for him, and the once sumptuous gardens did much as they pleased under the care of a single gardener. I think I must risk giving the gardener's real name, for none I could invent would have so appropriate a flavor. It was John Scripture, and he was assisted, from time to time, by an aged and lunatic father who, in his lucid intervals, would be let out from his captivity under the eaves of the lodge to putter amid the lewd topiarian extravagance of the hedges.

The doctor was to come down when he could, with a promise of some good golf, long nights of exquisite silence, and a ghost or two thrown in if his fancy ran that way. It was characteristic of his rather ponderous humor that, in writing to fix a day, he addressed Cazalet at "The Creeps, Sevenoaks, Kent." When he arrived, it was to find his host away from home and not due back until all hours. Barach was to dine alone with a reproachful setter for a companion, and not wait up. His bedroom on the ground floor was beautifully paneled from footboard to ceiling, but some misguided housekeeper under the fourth George had fallen upon the lovely woodwork with a can of black varnish. The dowry brought by a Cazalet bride of the mauve decade had been invested in a few vintage bathrooms, and one of these had replaced a prayer closet that once opened into this bedroom. There was only a candle to read by, but the light of a full moon came waveringly through the wind-stirred vines that half curtained the mullioned windows.

In this museum, Barach dropped off to sleep. He did not know how long he had slept when he found himself awake again, and conscious that something was astir in the room. It took him a moment to place the movement, but at last, in a patch of moonlight, he made out a hunched figure that seemed to be sitting with bent, engrossed head in the chair by the door. It was the hand, or rather the whole arm, that was moving, tracing a recurrent if irregular course in the air. At first the gesture was teasingly half-familiar, and then Barach recognized it as the one a woman makes when embroidering. There would be a hesitation as if the needle were being thrust through some taut, resistant material, and then, each time, the long, swift, sure pull of the thread.

To the startled guest, this seemed the least menacing activity he had ever heard ascribed to a ghost, but just the same he had only one idea, and that was to get out of that room with all possible dispatch. His mind made a hasty reconnaissance. The door into the hall was out of the question, for madness lay that way. At least he would have to pass right by that weaving arm. Nor did he relish a blind plunge into the thorny shrubbery beneath his window, and a barefoot scamper across the frosty turf. Of course, there was the bathroom, but that was small comfort if he could not get out of it by another door. In a spasm of concentration, he remembered that he *had* seen another door. Just at the moment of this realization, he heard the comfortingly actual sound of a car coming up the drive, and guessed that it was his host returning. In one magnificent movement, he leaped to the floor, bounded into the bathroom, and bolted its door behind him. The floor of the room beyond was quilted with moonlight. Wading through that, he arrived breathless, but unmolested, in the corridor. Further along he could see the lamp left burning in the entrance hall and hear the clatter of his host closing the front door.

As Barach came hurrying out of the darkness to greet him, Cazalet boomed his delight at such affability, and famished by his long, cold ride, proposed an immediate raid on the larder. The doctor, already sheepish at his recent panic, said nothing about it, and was all for food at once. With lighted candles held high, the foraging party descended on the offices, and mine host was descanting on the merits of cold roast beef, Cheddar cheese, and milk as a light midnight snack, when he stumbled over a bundle on the floor. With a cheerful curse at the old goody of the kitchen who was always leaving something about, he bent to see what it was this time, and let out a whistle of surprise. Then, by two candles held low, he and the doctor saw something they will not forget while they live. It was the body of the cook. Just the body. The head was gone. On the floor alongside lay a bloody cleaver.

"Old Scripture, by God!" Cazalet cried out, and, in a flash, Barach guessed. Still clutching a candle in one hand, he dragged his companion back through the interminable house to the room from which he had fled, motioning him to be silent, tiptoeing the final steps. That precaution was wasted, for a regiment could not have disturbed the rapt contentment of the ceremony still in progress within. The old lunatic had not left his seat by the door. Between his knees he still held the head of the woman he had killed. Scrupulously, happily, crooning at his work, he was plucking out the gray hairs one by one.

■John Collier

Evening Primrose

Love—especially romantic love—among the defunct? But, after all, the lover in this tale was a poet—and poets often dream of the impossible. Perhaps the locale is what makes it possible. So, the next time you are quietly browsing through your favorite department store—listen. You might hear "some wispy-sounding laughs, like the stridulations of the ghosts of grasshoppers!"

March 21. TODAY I MADE MY DECISION. I would turn my back for good and all upon the *bourgeois* world that hates a poet. I would leave, get out, break away—

And I have done it. I am free! Free as the mote that dances in the sunbeam! Free as my verse! Free as the food I shall eat, the paper I write upon, the lamb's-wool-lined softly slithering slippers I shall wear.

This morning I had not so much as a carfare. Now

59

I am here, on velvet. You are itching to learn of this haven; you would like to organize trips here, spoil it, send your relations-in-law, perhaps even come yourself. After all, this journal will hardly fall into your hands till I am dead. I'll tell you.

I am at Bracey's Giant Emporium, as happy as a mouse in the middle of an immense cheese, and the world shall know me no more.

Merrily, merrily shall I live now secure behind a towering pile of carpets, in a corner-nook which I propose to line with eiderdowns, angora vestments, and the Cleopatrean tops in pillows. I shall be cozy.

I nipped into this sanctuary late this afternoon, and soon heard the dying footballs of closing time. From now on, my only effort will be to dodge the night watchman. Poets can dodge.

I have already made my first mouselike exploration. I tiptoed as far as the stationery department, and, timid, darted back with only these writing materials, the poet's first need. Now I shall lay them aside, and seek other necessities: food, wine, the soft furniture of my couch, and a natty smoking jacket. This place stimulates me. I shall write here.

Dawn, next day. I suppose no one in the world was ever more astonished and overwhelmed than I have been tonight. It is unbelievable. Yet I believe it. How interesting life is when things get like that!

I crept out, as I said I would, and found the great shop in mingled light and gloom. The central well was half illuminated; the circling galleries towered in a pansy Piranesi of toppling light and shade. The spidery stairways and flying bridges had passed from purpose into fantasy. Silks and velvets glimmered like ghosts, a hundred pantie-clad models offered simpers and embraces to the desert air. Rings, clips, and bracelets glittered frostily in a desolate absence of Honey and Daddy.

Creeping along the transverse aisles, which were in deeper darkness, I felt like a wandering thought in the dreaming brain of a chorus girl down on her luck. Only, of course, their brains are not as big as Bracey's Giant Emporium. And there was no man there.

None, that is, except the night watchman. I had forgotten him. As I crossed an open space on the mezzanine floor, hugging the lee of a display of sultry shawls, I became aware of a regular thudding, which might almost have been that of my own heart. Suddenly it burst upon me that it came from outside. It was footsteps, and they were only a few paces away. Quick as a flash I seized a flamboyant mantilla, whirled it about me and stood with one arm outflung, like a Carmen petrified in a gesture of disdain.

I was successful. He passed me, jingling his little machine on its chain, humming his little tune, his eyes scaled with refractions of the blaring day. "Go, worldling!" I whispered, and permitted myself a soundless laugh.

It froze on my lips. My heart faltered. A new fear seized me.

I was afraid to move. I was afraid to look around. I felt I was being watched, by something that could see right through me. This was a very different feeling from the ordinary emergency caused by the very ordinary night watchman. My conscious impulse was the obvious one: to glance behind me. But my eyes knew better. I remained absolutely petrified, staring straight ahead.

My eyes were trying to tell me something that my brain refused to believe. They made their point. I was

61

looking straight into another pair of eyes, human eyes, but large, flat, luminous. I have seen such eyes among nocturnal creatures, which creep out under the artificial blue moonlight in the zoo.

The owner was only a dozen feet away from me. The watchman had passed between us, nearer him than me. Yet he had not seen him. I must have been looking straight at him for several minutes at a stretch. I had not seen him either.

He was half reclining against a low dais where, on a floor of russet leaves, and flanked by billows of glowing homespun, the fresh-faced waxen girls modeled spectator sports suits in herringbones, checks, and plaids. He leaned against the skirt of one of these Dianas; its folds concealed perhaps his ear, his shoulder, and a little of his right side. He, himself, was clad in dim but large-patterned Shetland tweeds of the latest cut, suede shoes, a shirt of a rather broad *motif* in olive, pink, and gray. He was as pale as a creature found under a stone. His long thin arms ended in hands that hung gloatingly, more like trailing, transparent fins, or wisps of chiffon, than ordinary hands.

He spoke. His voice was not a voice; it was a mere whistling under the tongue. "Not bad, for a beginner!"

I grasped that he was complimenting me, rather satirically, on my own, more amateurish, feat of camouflage. I stuttered. I said, "I'm sorry. I didn't know anyone else lived here." I noticed, even as I spoke, that I was imitating his own whistling sibilant utterance.

"Oh, yes," he said. *"We* live here. It's delightful."

"We?"

"Yes, all of us. Look!"

62

We were near the edge of the first gallery. He swept his long hand round, indicating the whole well of the shop. I looked. I saw nothing. I could hear nothing, except the watchman's thudding step receding infinitely far along some basement aisle.

"Don't you see?"

You know the sensation one has, peering into the half-light of a vivarium? One sees bark, pebbles, a few leaves, nothing more. And then, suddenly, a stone breathes—it is a toad; there is a chameleon, another, a coiled adder, a mantis among the leaves. The whole case seems crepitant with life. Perhaps the whole world is. One glances at one's sleeve, one's feet.

So it was with the shop. I looked, and it was empty. I looked, and there was an old lady, clambering out from behind the monstrous clock. There were three girls, elderly *ingenues,* incredibly emaciated, simpering at the entrance of the perfumery. Their hair was a fine floss, pale as gossamer. Equally brittle and colorless was a man with the appearance of a colonel of southern extraction, who stood regarding me while he caressed mustachios that would have done credit to a crystal shrimp. A chintzy woman, possibly of literary tastes, swam forward from the curtains and drapes.

They came thick about me, fluttering, whistling, like a waving of gauze in the wind. Their eyes were wide and flatly bright. I saw there was no color to the iris.

"How raw he looks!"

"A detective! Send for the Dark Men!"

"I'm not a detective. I am a poet. I have renounced the world."

"He is a poet. He has come over to us. Mr. Roscoe found him."

63

"He admires us."

"He must meet Mrs. Vanderpant."

I was taken to meet Mrs. Vanderpant. She proved to be the Grand Old Lady of the store, almost entirely transparent.

"So you are a poet, Mr. Snell? You will find inspiration here. I am quite the oldest inhabitant. Three mergers and a complete rebuilding, but they didn't get rid of *me!*"

"Tell how you went out by daylight, dear Mrs. Vanderpant, and nearly got bought for Whistler's *Mother!*"

"That was in prewar days. I was more robust then. But at the cash desk they suddenly remembered there was no frame. And when they came back to look at me—"

"—She was gone."

Their laughter was like the stridulation of the ghosts of grasshoppers.

"Where is Ella? Where is my broth?"

"She is bringing it, Mrs. Vanderpant. It will come."

"Tiresome little creature! She is our foundling, Mr. Snell. She is not quite our sort."

"Is that so, Mrs. Vanderpant? Dear, dear!"

"I lived alone here, Mr. Snell, for many years. I took refuge here in the terrible times in the eighties. I was a young girl then, a beauty, people were kind enough to say, but poor Papa lost his money. Bracey's meant a lot to a young girl, in the New York of those days, Mr. Snell. It seemed to me terrible that I should not be able to come here in the ordinary way. So I came here for good. I was quite alarmed when others began to come in, after the crash of 1907. But it was the dear Judge, the Colonel, Mrs. Bilbee—"

I bowed. I was being introduced.

"Mrs. Bilbee writes plays. *And* of a very old

64

Philadelphia family. You will find us quite *nice* here, Mr. Snell."

"I feel it a great privilege, Mrs. Vanderpant."

"And of course, all our dear *young* people came in '29. *Their* poor papas jumped from skyscrapers."

I did a great deal of bowing and whistling. The introductions took a long time. Who would have thought so many people lived in Bracey's?

"And here at last is Ella with my broth."

It was then I noticed that the young people were not so young after all, in spite of their smiles, their little ways, their *ingenue* dress. Ella was in her teens. Clad only in something from the shop-soiled counter, she nevertheless had the appearance of a living flower in a French cemetery, or a mermaid among polyps.

"Come, you stupid thing!"

"Mrs. Vanderpant is waiting."

Her pallor was not like theirs; not like the pallor of something that glistens or scuttles when you turn over a stone. Hers was that of a pearl.

Ella! Pearl of this remotest, most fantastic cave! Little mermaid, brushed over, pressed down by objects of a deadlier white—tentacles—! I can write no more.

March 28. Well, I am rapidly becoming used to my new and half-lit world, to my strange company. I am learning the intricate laws of silence and camouflage which dominate the apparently casual strolling and gatherings of the midnight clan. How they detest the night watchman, whose existence imposes these laws on their idle festivals!

"Odious, vulgar creature! He reeks of the coarse sun!"

Actually, he is quite a personable young man, very

young for a night watchman, so young that I think he must have been wounded in the war. But they would like to tear him to pieces.

They are very pleasant to me, though. They are pleased that a poet should have come among them. Yet I cannot like them entirely. My blood is a little chilled by the uncanny ease with which even the old ladies can clamber spiderlike from balcony to balcony. Or is it because they are unkind to Ella?

Yesterday we had a bridge party. Tonight, Mrs. Bilbee's little play, *Love in Shadowland,* is going to be presented. Would you believe it?—another colony, from Wanamaker's, is coming over *en masse* to attend. Apparently people live in all the great stores. This visit is considered a great honor, for there is an intense snobbery in these creatures. They speak with horror of a social outcast who left a high-class Madison Avenue establishment, and now leads a wallowing, beachcomberish life in a delicatessen. And they relate with tragic emotion the story of the man in Altman's, who conceived such a passion for a model plaid dressing jacket that he emerged and wrested it from the hands of a purchaser.

April 14. I have found an opportunity to speak to Ella. I dared not before; here one has a sense always of pale eyes secretly watching. But last night, at the play, I developed a fit of hiccups. I was somewhat sternly told to go and secrete myself in the basement, among the garbage cans, where the watchman never comes.

There, in the rat-haunted darkness, I heard a stifled sob. "What's that? Is it you? Is it Ella? What ails you, child? Why do you cry?"

"They wouldn't even let me see the play."

"Is that all? Let me console you."

66

"I am so unhappy."

She told me her tragic little story. What do you think? When she was a child, a little tiny child of only six, she strayed away and fell asleep behind a counter, while her mother tried on a new hat. When she awoke, the store was in darkness.

"And I cried, and they all came around, and took hold of me. 'She will tell, if we let her go,' they said. Some said, 'Call in the Dark Men.' 'Let her stay here,' said Mrs. Vanderpant. 'She will make me a nice little maid.'"

"Who are these Dark Men, Ella? They spoke of them when I came here."

"Don't you know? Oh, it's horrible! It's horrible!"

"Tell me, Ella. Let me share it."

She trembled. "You know the morticians, 'Journey's End,' who go to houses when people die?"

"Yes, Ella."

"Well, in that shop, just like here, and at Gimbel's, and at Bloomingdale's, there are people living, people like these."

"How disgusting! But what can they live upon, Ella, in a funeral home?"

"Don't ask me! Dead people are sent there, to be embalmed. Oh, they are terrible creatures! Even the people here are terrified of them. But if anyone dies, or if some poor burglar breaks in, and sees these people, and might tell—"

"Yes? Go on."

"Then they send for the others, the Dark Men."

"Good heavens!"

"Yes, and they put the body in Surgical Supplies— or the burglar, all tied up, if it's a burglar—and they send for these others, and then they all hide, and in they come, the others—Oh! they're like pieces of blackness. I saw them once. It was terrible."

67

"And then?"

"They go in, to where the dead person is, or the poor burglar. And they have wax there—and all sorts of things. And when they're gone there's just one of these wax models left, on the table. And then our people put a dress on it, or a bathing suit, and they mix it up with all the others, and nobody ever knows."

"But aren't they heavier than the others, these wax models? You would think they'd be heavier."

"No. They're not heavier. I think there's a lot of them—gone."

"Oh, dear! So they were going to do that to you, when you were a little child?"

"Yes, only Mrs. Vanderpant said I was to be her maid."

"I don't like these people, Ella."

"Nor do I. I wish I could see a bird."

"Why don't you go into the pet shop?"

"It wouldn't be the same. I want to see it on a twig, with leaves."

May 1. For the last few nights the store has been feverish with the shivering whisper of a huge crush at Bloomingdale's. Tonight was the night.

"Not changed yet? We leave on the stroke of two." Roscoe has appointed himself, or been appointed, my guide or my guard.

"Roscoe, I am still a greenhorn. I dread the streets."

"Nonsense! There's nothing to it. We slip out by twos and threes, stand on the sidewalk, pick up a taxi. Were you never out late in the old days? If so, you must have seen us, many a time."

"Good heavens, I believe I have! And often wondered where you came from. And it was from here! But Roscoe, my brow is burning. I find it hard to breathe. I fear a cold."

"In that case you must certainly remain behind. Our whole party would be disgraced in the unfortunate event of a sneeze."

I had relied on their rigid etiquette, so largely based on fear of discovery, and I was right. Soon they were gone, drifting out like leaves aslant on the wind. At once I dressed in flannel slacks, canvas shoes, and a tasteful sport shirt, all new in stock today. I found a quiet spot, safely off the track beaten by the night watchman. There in a model's lifted hand, I set a wide fern frond culled from the florist's shop, and at once had a young, spring tree. The carpet was sandy, sandy as a lake-side beach. A snowy napkin; two cakes, each with a cherry on it; I had only to imagine the lake and to find Ella.

"Why, Charles, what's this?"

"I'm a poet, Ella, and when a poet meets a girl like you he thinks of a day in the country. Do you see this tree? Let's call it our tree. There's the lake—the prettiest lake imaginable. Here is grass, and there are flowers. There are birds, too, Ella. You told me you like birds."

"Oh, Charles, you're so sweet. I feel I hear them singing."

"And here's our lunch. But before we eat, go behind the rock there, and see what you find."

I heard her cry out in delight when she saw the summer dress I had put there for her. When she came back the spring day smiled to see her, and the lake shone brighter than before. "Ella, let us have lunch. Let us have fun. Let us have a swim. I can just imagine you in one of those new bathing suits."

"Let's just sit there, Charles, and talk."

So we sat and talked, and the time was gone like a

dream. We might have stayed there, forgetful of everything, had it not been for the spider.

"Charles, what are you doing?"

"Nothing, my dear. Just a naughty little spider, crawling over your knee. Purely imaginary, of course, but that sort are sometimes the worst. I had to try to catch him."

"Don't Charles! It's late. It's terribly late. They'll be back any minute. I'd better go home."

I took her home to the kitchenware on the sub-ground floor, and kissed her good-day. She offered me her cheek. This troubles me.

May 10. "Ella, I love you."

I said it to her just like that. We have met many times. I have dreamed of her by day. I have not even kept up my journal. Verse has been out of the question.

"Ella, I love you. Let us move into the trousseau department. Don't look so dismayed, darling. If you like, we will go right away from here. We will live in that little restaurant in Central Park. There are thousands of birds there."

"Please—please don't talk like that!"

"But I love you with all my heart."

"You mustn't."

"But I find I must. I can't help it. Ella, you don't love another?"

She wept a little. "Oh, Charles, I do."

"Love another, Ella? One of these? I thought you dreaded them all. It must be Roscoe. He is the only one that's any way human. We talk of art, life, and such things. And he has stolen your heart!"

"No, Charles, no. He's just like the rest, really. I hate them all. They make me shudder."

"Who is it, then?"

"It's him."

"Who?"

"The night watchman."

"Impossible!"

"No. He smells of the sun."

"Oh, Ella, you have broken my heart."

"Be my friend, though."

"I will. I'll be your brother. How did you fall in love with him?"

"Oh, Charles, it was so wonderful. I was thinking of birds, and I was careless. Don't tell on me, Charles. They'll punish me."

"No, no. Go on."

"I was careless, and there he was, coming round the corner. And there was no place for me; I had this blue dress on. There were only some wax models in their underthings."

"Please go on."

"I couldn't help it. I slipped off my dress, and stood still."

"I see."

"And he stopped just by me, Charles. And he looked at me. And he touched my cheek."

"Did he notice nothing?"

"No. It was cold. But Charles, he said—he said— 'Say, honey, I wish they made 'em like you on Eighth Avenue.' Charles, wasn't that a lovely thing to say?"

"Personally, I should have said Park Avenue."

"Oh, Charles, don't get like these people here. Sometimes I think you're getting like them. It doesn't matter what street, Charles; it was a lovely thing to say."

"Yes, but my heart's broken. And what can you do about him? Ella, he belongs to another world."

"Yes, Charles, Eighth Avenue. I want to go there. Charles, are you truly my friend?"

"I'm your brother, only my heart's broken."

"I'll tell you. I will. I'm going to stand there again. So he'll see me."

"And then?"

"Perhaps he'll speak to me again."

"My dearest Ella, you are torturing yourself. You are making it worse."

"No, Charles. Because I shall answer him. He will take me away."

"Ella, I can't bear it."

"Ssh! There is someone coming. I shall see the birds—real birds, Charles—and flowers growing. They're coming. You must go."

May 13. The last three days have been torture. This evening I broke. Roscoe had joined me. He sat eyeing me for a long time. He put his hand on my shoulder.

He said, "You're looking seedy, old fellow. Why don't you go over to Wanamaker's for some skiing?"

His kindness compelled a frank response. "It's deeper than that, Roscoe. I'm done for. I can't eat. I can't sleep. I can't write, man, I can't even write."

"What is it? Day starvation?"

"Roscoe—it's love."

"Not one of the staff, Charles, or the customers? That's absolutely forbidden."

"No, it's not that, Roscoe. But just as hopeless."

"My dear fellow, I can't bear to see you like this. Let me help you. Let me share your trouble."

Then it all came out. It burst out. I trusted him. I think I trusted him. I really think I had no intention of betraying Ella, of spoiling her escape, of keeping her here till her heart turned towards me. If I had, it was subconscious, I swear it.

But I told him all. All! He was sympathetic, but I detected a sly reserve in his sympathy. "You will

72

respect my confidence, Roscoe? This is to be a secret between us."

"As secret as the grave, old chap."

And he must have gone straight to Mrs. Vanderpant. This evening the atmosphere has changed. People flicker to and fro, smiling nervously, horribly, with a sort of frightened sadistic exaltation. When I speak to them they answer evasively, fidget, and disappear. An informal dance has been called off. I cannot find Ella. I will creep out. I will look for her again.

Later. Heaven! It has happened. I went in desperation to the manager's office, whose glass front overlooks the whole shop. I watched till midnight. Then I saw a little group of them, like ants bearing a victim. They were carrying Ella. They took her to the Surgical Department. They took other things.

And, coming back here, I was passed by a flittering, whispering horde of them, glancing over their shoulders in a thrilled ecstasy of panic, making for their hiding places. I, too, hid myself. How can I describe the dark inhuman creatures that passed me, silent as shadows? They went there—where Ella is.

What can I do? There is only one thing. I will find the watchman. I will tell him. He and I will save her. And if we are overpowered— Well, I will leave this on a counter. Tomorrow, if we live, I can recover it.

If not, look in the windows. Look for three new figures: two men, one rather sensitive-looking, and a girl. She has blue eyes, like periwinkle flowers, and her upper lip is lifted a little.

Look for us.

Smoke them out! Obliterate them! Avenge us!

73

▪E. F. Benson

The Step

The imagination has no dearth of creatures it can conjure up to bedevil our lives. Sometimes they come in the form of sleep demons as we lie in the security of our beds, sometimes they come as sun-blinding hallucinatory figures as we cross a desert of emotional turmoil. Sometimes they come under more ordinary circumstances—the more terrifying because of their banality.

JOHN CRESSWELL was returning home one night from the Britannia Club at Alexandria, where, as was his custom three or four times in the week, he had dined very solidly and fluidly, and played bridge afterward as long as a table could be formed. It had been rather an expensive evening, for all his skill at cards had been unable to cope with such a continuous series of ill-favored hands as had been his. But he had consoled himself with reasonable doses of

75

whiskey, and now he stepped homeward in very cheerful spirits, for his business affairs were going most prosperously and a loss of twenty-five or thirty pounds tonight would be amply compensated for in the morning. Besides, his bridge-account for the year showed a credit which proved that cards were a very profitable pleasure.

It was a hot night in October, and, being a big, plethoric man, he strolled at a very leisurely pace across the square and up the long street at the far end of which was his house. There were no taxis on the rank, or he would have taken one and saved himself this walk of nearly a mile; but he had no quarrel with that, for the night air with a breeze from the sea was refreshing after so long a session in a smoke-laden atmosphere. Above, a moon near to its full cast a very clear white light on his road. There was a narrow strip of sharp-cut shadow beneath the houses on his right, but the rest of the street and the pavement on the left of it, where he walked, were in bright illumination.

At first his way lay between rows of shops, European for the most part, with here and there a café where a few customers still lingered. Pleasant thoughts beguiled his progress; the Egyptian sugar crop, in which he was much interested, had turned out very well and he saw a big profit on his options. Not less satisfactory were other businesses in which he did not figure so openly. He lent money, for instance, on a large scale, to the native population, and these operations extended far up the Nile. Only last week he had been at Luxor, where he had concluded a transaction of a very remunerative sort. He had made a loan some months ago to a small merchant there and now the appropriate interest on this was in default: in consequence the harvest of a very fruitful acreage of sugarcane was his. A similar and even richer windfall had just come his way in Alexandria, for he had advanced money a year ago to a Levantine tobacco merchant on the security of his freehold store. This had brought him in very handsome interest, but a day or two ago the unfortunate fellow had failed, and Cresswell owned a most desirable freehold. The whole affair had been very creditable to his enterprise and sagacity, for he had privately heard that the municipality was intending to lay out the neighborhood, a slum at present, where this store was situated, in houses of flats, and make it a residential quarter, and his newly acquired freehold would thus become a valuable property.

At present the tobacco merchant lived with his family in holes and corners of the store, and they must be evicted tomorrow morning. John Cresswell had already arranged for this, and had told the man that he would have to quit: he would go round there in the forenoon and see that they and their sticks of furniture were duly bundled out into the street. He would see personally that this was done, and looked forward to doing so. The old couple were beastly creatures, the woman a perfect witch who eyed him and muttered, but there was a daughter who was not ill-looking, and someone of the beggared family would be obliged to earn bread. He did not dwell on this, but the thought just flitted through his brain. . . . Then doors would be locked and windows barred in the store that was now his, and he would lunch at the club afterwards. He was popular there; he had a jovial geniality about him, and a habit of offering drinks before they could be offered to him. That, too, was good for business.

Ten minutes' strolling brought him to the end of

the shops and cafés that formed the street, and now the road ran between residential houses, each detached and with a space of garden surrounding it, where dry-leaved palms rattled in this wind from the sea. He was approaching the flamboyant Roman Catholic church, to which was attached a monastic establishment, a big white barrack-looking house where the Brothers of Poverty or some such order lived. Something to do with St. Mark, he vaguely remembered, who by tradition had brought Christianity to Egypt nearly nineteen hundred years ago. Often he met one of these odd sandal-footed creatures with his brown habit, his rosary and his cowled head going in or out of their gate, or toiling in their garden. He did not like them: lousy fellows he would have called them. Sometimes in their mendicant errands they came to his door asking alms for the indigent Copts. Not long ago he had found one actually ringing the bell of his front door, instead of going humbly round to the back, as befitted his quality, and Cresswell told him that he would loose his bulldog on the next of their breed who ventured within his garden gate. How the fellow had skipped off when he heard talk of the dog! He dropped one of his sandals in his haste to be gone, and not sparing the time to adjust it again, had hopped and hobbled over the sharp gravel to gain the street. Cresswell had laughed aloud to see his precipitancy, and the best of the joke was that he had not got any sort of dog on his premises at all. At the remembrance of that humorous incident he grinned to himself as he passed the porch of the church.

He paused a moment to mop his forehead and to light a cigarette, looking about him in great good humor. Before him and behind the road was quite empty: lights gleamed behind venetian shutters from a few upper windows of the houses, but all the world was in bed or on its way there. There were still three or four hundred yards to go before he came to his house, and as he turned his face homeward again and walked a little more briskly, he heard a step behind him, sharp and distinct, not far in his rear. He paid no heed: someone, late like himself, was going home, walking in the same direction, for the step followed him.

His cigarette was ill-lit; a little core of burning stuff fell from it onto the pavement and he stopped to rekindle it. Possibly some subconscious region of his mind was occupied with the step which had sprung up so oddly behind him in the empty street, for while he was getting his cigarette to burn again he noticed that the step had ceased. It was hardly worthwhile to turn around (so little the matter interested him), but a casual glance showed him that the wayfarer must have turned into one of the houses he had just passed, for the whole street, brightly moonlit, was as empty as when he surveyed it a few minutes before. Soon he came to his own gate and clanged it behind him.

The eviction of the Levantine merchant took place in the morning, and Cresswell watched his porters carrying out the tawdry furniture—a few tables, a few chairs, a sofa covered in tattered crimson plush, a couple of iron bedsteads, a bundle of dirty sheets and blankets. He was not certain in his own mind whether these paltry articles did not by rights belong to him, but they were fit for nothing except the dustheap, and he had no use for them. There they stood in the clean bright sunshine, rubbish and no more, blocking the pavement, and a policeman told their owner that he had best clear them away at once unless he wanted trouble. There was the usual scene to which he was quite accustomed: the man's wife sniveling and slovenly, witchlike and early old, knelt and kissed his hand, and wheezingly besought his compassion. She called him "Excellency," she promised him her prayers, which he desired as little as her pots and pans. She invoked blessings on his head, for she knew that out of his pity he would give them a little more time. They had nowhere to go nor any roof to shelter them: her husband had money owing to him, and he would collect these debts and pay his default as sure as there was a God in heaven. This was a changed note from her mutterings of yesterday, but of course Cresswell had a deaf ear for this oily rigmarole, and presently he went into the store to see that everything had been removed.

It was in a filthy, dirty state; floors were rotten and the paint peeling, but the whole place would soon be broken up and he was not going to spend a piaster on it, so long as the ground on which it stood was his. Then he saw to the barring of the windows and the doors, and he gave the policeman quite a handsome tip to keep an eye on the place and take care that these folk did not get ingress again. When he came out, he found that the old man had procured a handcart, and he and his son were loading it up, so of course they had somewhere to go: it was all a pack of lies about their being homeless. The old hag was squatting against the house wall, but now there were no more prayers and blessings for him, and she had taken to her mutterings again. As for the daughter, seen in the broad daylight, she had a handsome face, but she was sullen and dirty and forbidding, and he gave no further thought to her. He hailed a taxi and went off to the club for lunch.

Though Cresswell, in common parlance, "did himself well," taking his fill of food and drink and tobacco, he was also careful of that great strong body of his, and the occasions were few when he omitted, at the end of the day's work, to walk out in the direction of Ramleh for a brisk hour or two, or, during the hotter months, to have a good swim in the sea and a bask in the sun. On the day following this eviction he took a tramp along the firm sands of the coast, and then, turning inland, struck the road that would bring him back to his own house. This stood quite at the end of the rows of detached houses past which he had walked two evenings before: beyond, the road ran between tumbled sand-dunes and scrub-covered flats. Here and there in sheltered hollows a few Arab goat-herds and such had made themselves nomadic tentlike habitations of a primitive sort: half a dozen posts set in the sand supported a roof of rugs and blankets stitched together. If they encroached too near the outskirts of the town the authorities periodically made a clearance of them, for they were apt to be light-fingered, pilfering folk, whose close vicinity was not desirable.

Today as he returned from his walk, Cresswell saw that a tent of this kind had newly been set up within twenty yards of his own garden wall. That would not do at all, that must be seen to, and he determined as soon as he had had his bath and his change of clothes to ring up his very good friend the chief inspector of police and request its removal. As he got nearer to it he saw that it was not quite of the usual type. The roof was clearly an outworn European carpet, and standing outside it on the sand were chairs and a sofa. Somehow these seemed familiar to him, though he could not localize the association. Then out of the tent came that old Levantine hag who had kissed his hand and knelt to him yesterday, invoking on him all sorts of blessings and

81

prosperities, if only he would have compassion. She saw him, for now not more than a few dozen yards separated them, and then, suddenly pointing at him, she broke out into a gabble and yell of curses. That made him smile.

"So you've changed your tune again, have you?" he thought, "for that doesn't sound much like good wishes. Curse away, old woman, if it relieves your mind, for it doesn't hurt me. But you'll have to be shifting once more, for I'm not having you and your like squatting there."

Cresswell rang up his friend the chief inspector of police, and was most politely told that the matter should be seen to in the morning. Sure enough, when he set out to go to his office next day, he saw that it was being attended to, for the European carpet which had served for a roof was already down, and the handcart was being laden with the stuff. He noticed, quite casually, that the two women and the boy were employed in loading it; the Levantine was lying on the sand and taking no part in the work. Two days later he had occasion to pass the pauper cemetery of Alexandria, where the poorest kind of funeral was going on. The coffin was being pushed to the side of the shallow grave on a handcart: a boy and two women followed it. He could see who they were.

He dined that night at the club in rare good humor with the affairs of life. Already the municipality had offered him for his newly acquired freehold a sum that was double the debt for which it had been security, and though possibly he might get more if he stuck out for a higher price, he had accepted it, and the money had been paid into his bank that day. To get a hundred per cent in a week was very satisfactory business, and who knew but that some new scheme of improvement might cause them to change their plans, leaving him with a ramshackle building on his hands for which he had no manner of use? He enjoyed his dinner and his wine, and particularly did he enjoy the rubber of bridge that followed. All went well with his finesses; he doubled his adversaries two or three times with the happiest results, they doubled him and were sorry for having spoken, and there would be a very pleasant item to enter in his card account that evening.

It was later than usual when he quitted the club. Just outside there was a beggar woman squatting at the edge of the pavement, who held her palm toward him and whined out blessings. Good-naturedly he fumbled in his pocket for a couple of piasters, and the blessings poured out in greater shrillness and copiousness as she pushed back the black veil that half shrouded her face to thank him for his beneficence to the needy widow. Next moment she threw his alms on the pavement, she spat at him, and like a moth she flitted away into the shadows.

Cresswell recognized her even as she had recognized him, and picked up his piasters. It was amusing to think that the old hag so hated him that even his alms were abhorrent to her. "I'll drop them into that collecting box outside the church," he thought to himself.

Tonight, late though it was, there were many folk about in the square, natives for the most part, padding softly along, and there were still a few taxis on the rank. But he preferred to walk home, for he had been so busy all day that he had given his firm fat body no sort of exercise. So, crossing the square, he went up the street which led to his house. Here the cafés were already closed, and soon the pavements grew empty. The waning moon had risen, and though the lights of the street grew more sparse as he emerged into the residential quarter, his way lay bright before him. In his hand he still held the two piasters which had been flung back at him, ready for the collection box. He walked briskly, for the night was cool, and it was no exercise to saunter. Not a breath of wind stirred the air, and the clatter of the dry palm leaves was dumb.

He was now approaching the Roman Catholic church, when a step suddenly sounded out crisp and distinct behind him. He remembered then for the first time what had happened some nights ago and halted and listened: not a sound broke the stillness. He whisked around, but the street seemed empty. On he went again, now more slowly, and there was the following step again, neither gaining on him nor falling behind; to judge by the loudness of it, it could not be more than a dozen paces in his rear. Then a very obvious explanation occurred to him: no doubt this was some echo of his own footsteps. He went more quickly, and the steps behind him quickened; he stopped and they stopped. The whole thing was clear enough, and not a shadow of uneasiness, or anything approaching it, was in his mind. He slipped his ironical alms into the collecting box outside the church, and was amused to hear that they evoked no tinkle from within. "Quite a little windfall for those brown-gowned fellows; they'll buy another rosary," he said to himself, and soon, with the echo of his own steps following, he turned in at his gate. Once inside, he slipped behind a myrtle bush that stood at the edge of the gravel walk, to see if by chance anyone passed on the road outside. But nothing happened, and this theory of the echo, though it was odd that he should never have noticed it till so lately, seemed quite confirmed.

From that night onward he made it a practice, if he

dined at the club, to walk home. Sometimes the step followed him, but not always, and this was an objection to that sensible echo theory. But the matter was no sort of worry to him except sometimes when he woke in the night and found that his brain, still drowsy and not in complete control, was brooding over it with an ever-increasing preoccupation. Often that misgiving faded away and he dropped off to dreamless sleep again; sometimes it was sufficiently disquieting to bring him fully awake, and then with all his senses about him, it vanished. But there was this condition, halfway between waking and sleeping, when in the twilight chamber of his brain something listened, something feared. When fully awake he no more thought of it than he thought of that frowsy Levantine tobacco merchant whom he had evicted and whose funeral he chanced to have seen.

Early in December his cousin and partner in the sugar business came down from Cairo to spend a week with him. Bill Cresswell may be succinctly described as "a hot lot," and often after dinner at the club he left his cousin to his cronies and the sedater pleasures of bridge, and went out with a duplicate latchkey in his pocket on livelier private affairs. One night, the last of Bill's sojourn here, there was "nothing doing," and the two set forth together homeward from the club.

"Nice night, let's walk," said John. "Nothing like a walk when there's liquid on board. Clears the brain, for you and I must have a final powwow tonight, if you're off tomorrow. There are some bits of things still to go through."

Bill acquiesced. The cafés were all closed, there was nothing very promising.

"Night life here ain't a patch on Cairo," he

observed. "Everyone seems to go to bed here just about when we begin to get going. Not but what I haven't enjoyed my stay with you. Capital good fellows at your club, and brandy to match."

He stopped and ruefully scanned the quiet and emptiness of the street.

"Not a soul anywhere," he said. "Shutters up, all gone to bed. Nothing for it but a powwow, I guess."

They walked on in silence for a while. Then behind them, firm and distinct to John's ears, there sprang up the sound of the footsteps, for which now he knew that he waited and listened. He wheeled around.

"What's up?" asked Bill.

"Curious thing," said John. "Night after night now, though not every night, when I walk home, I hear a step following me. I heard it then."

Bill gave a vinous giggle.

"No such luck for me," he said. "I like to hear a step following me about one of a morning. Something agreeable may come of it. Wish *I* could hear it."

They walked on, and again, clearer than before, John heard what was inaudible to the other. He told himself, as he often did now, that it was an echo. But it was odd that the echo only repeated the footfalls of one of them. As he recognized this, he felt for the first time, when he was fully awake, some sudden chill of fear. It was as if a cold hand closed for a moment on his heart, just pressing it softly, almost tenderly. But they were now close to his own gate, and presently it clanged behind them.

Bill returned the next day to the gladder life of Cairo. John Cresswell saw him off at the station and was passing out into the street again through the crowd of loungers and porters and passengers when there defined itself to his ear the sound of that footstep which he knew so well. How he recognized it and isolated it from the tread of so many other feet he had no idea: simply his brain told him that it was following him again. He took a taxi to his office, and as he mounted the white stone stairs once more it was on his track. Once more the gentle pressure of cold fingers seemed to assure him of the presence that, though invisible, was very close to him, and now it was as if those fingers were pressed on some bell-push in his brain, and there sounded out a shrill tingle of fear. So hardheaded and sensible a man, of course, had nothing but scorn for all the clap-trap bogey tales of spirits and ghosts and hauntings, and he would have welcomed any sort of apparition in which the step manifested itself, in order to have the pleasure of laughing in its face. He would have liked to see a skeleton or some shrouded figure stand close to him; he would have slashed at it with his stick and convinced himself that there was nothing there. Whatever his own eyes appeared to see could not be so unnerving as these tokens of the invisible.

A stiff drink pulled him together again, and for the rest of the day there occurred no repetition of that tapping step which had begun to sprout with terror for him. In any case he was determined to fight it, for he realized that it was chiefly his own fear that troubled him. No doubt he was suffering from some small nervous derangement; he had been working very hard, and after Christmas, if the thing continued to worry him, probably he would see a doctor, who would prescribe him some tonic or some sedative which would send the step into the limbo from which it had come. But it was more probable that his cure was in his own hands: his own resistance was all the medicine he needed.

It was in pursuance of this very sane policy that he set out that night after an evening at the club to walk home: he faced it just because he knew that some black well was digging itself into his soul. To yield, to take a taxi, was to retreat, and if he did that, if he gave way an inch, he guessed that he might be soon flying in panic before an invading and imaginary host of phantoms. He had no use for phantoms; the solid satisfactions of life were enough occupation. Once more, as he drew near the church, the step sprang up, and now he sought no longer to tell himself it was an echo. Instead he fixed his mind on it, saying to himself, "There it is and it can't hurt me. Let it walk all day and night behind me if it chooses. It's got a fancy for me." Then his garden gate shut behind him, and with a sigh of relief he knew that he had passed out of its beat, for when once he was within, it never came farther.

He stood for a moment on his threshold, after he had opened his door, pleased with himself for having faced it. The bright light shone full onto the straight gravel walk he had just traversed. It was quite empty, and nothing was looking in through his gate. Then he heard from close at hand the crunch of the gravel underneath the heel of some invisible wayfarer. Now was the time to assert himself again, to look his fear in the eyes and mock at it.

"Come along, whoever you are," he called, "and have a drink before you get back to hell. Something cooling. Drop of cold water, isn't it?"

Thick sweat had broken out on his forehead, and his hand on the doorknob shook as with ague as he stood there looking out onto the bright empty path. But he did not flinch from the lesson he was teaching himself. The seconds ticked away: he could count them from the pulse that hammered in his throat. "I'll give it a hundred beats," he said to himself, "and then I'll say good night to Mr. Nothing-at-all."

He counted his hundred, he gave ten beats more for good luck. "Good night, you old fraud," he said, and went in and secured the door.

It seemed indeed for the week that followed that he had rightly gauged the nature of the hallucination which had threatened to establish its awful dominion over him. Never once, whether by day or night, did there come to his ears that footfall which he feared and listened for, nor, if in the dead hours of the darkness he lay for a while between sleep and waking, did he quake with a sense that something unseen and aware was watching him. A little courage, a flat denial of his fears had been sufficient not only to scotch them, but to snuff out the manifestation which had caused them. He kept his thoughts well in hand, he would not even conjecture what had been the cause of that visitation. Occasionally, while it still vexed him, he had cast about for the origin of it, he had wondered whether that shrill Levantine hag calling curses on him could somehow have found root in his mind. But now it was past and done with: he would have a few days' remission from work, if it was overwork that had been at the bottom of it, at Christmas, and perhaps it would be prudent not to be quite so free with the club brandy.

On Christmas Eve he and his friends sat at their bridge till close on midnight, then lingered over a drink, wished each other seasonable greetings and dispersed. Cresswell hesitated as to whether he should not take a taxi home, for the object with which he had trudged back there so often seemed to be gained, and he no longer feared the recurrence of the step. But he thought he would just set the seal on his victory and went on foot.

He had come to the point in his walk where he had first heard the step. Tonight, as usual, there was none, and he stopped for a moment looking around him securely and serenely. It was a bright night, luminous with a moon a little after the full, and it amazed him to think that he had ever fashioned a terror to himself in this quiet, orderly street. From not far ahead there came the sound of the bells of the church saluting Christmas morning. They would have been holding their midnight Mass there. He breathed the night air with content, and throwing the butt of his spent cigar into the roadway, he walked on again.

With a sudden sinking of his heart, he heard behind him the step which he thought he had silenced forever. It was faint at first, but tonight, instead of keeping at a uniform distance behind him, it was approaching. Louder and more crisp it sounded, until it was close to him. On and on it came, still gaining on him, and now there brushed by him, though not quite touching him, the figure of a man in European dress, with his head wrapped in a shawl.

"Hello, you there," called Cresswell. "You're the skunk who's been following me, are you, and slipping out of sight again? No more of your damned conjuring tricks. Let's have a look at you."

The figure, now some two or three yards ahead of him, stopped at the sound of his voice and turned around. The shawl covered its face, but for a narrow chink between the edges.

"So you understand English," said Cresswell. "Now I'll thank you to take that shawl off your face, and let me see who it is that's been dogging me."

The man raised his hands and threw back the shawl. The moonlight shone on his face, and that face was just a slab of smooth yellowish flesh extending from ear to ear, empty as the oval of an

90

egg without eyes or nose or mouth. From the upper edge of the shawl where it crossed the forehead there depended a few wisps of gray hair.

Cresswell looked, and a wave of panic fear submerged his very soul. He gave a little thin squeal and started to run, listening the while in an agony of terror to hear if the steps of that nameless, faceless creature were following. He must run, he must run, to get away from that thing out of hell which had manifested itself.

Then close at hand he saw the lights of the church, and there perhaps he could find sanctuary from it. The door was open, and he sprang up the steps. Close by there were lights burning on the altar of a side chapel, and he flung himself on his knees. Not for years had he attempted to pray, and now in the agony of his soul he could but say in a gabbling whisper, 'O my God, O my God." Over and over he said it.

By degrees some sort of self-control came back to him. There were holy images, there was a sacred picture above the altar, a smell of hallowing incense was in the air. Surely there was protection here, a power that would intervene between him and the terror of that face. A sort of tranquillity overscored his panic, and he began to look around.

The church was darker than it had been when he entered, and he saw that some of those cowled brown-habited men of the order were moving quietly about, quenching the lights. Those at the altar in front of which he knelt were still bright, and now he saw one of these cowled figures move up close to him, as if waiting for him to finish his devotions. He was calm now, his panic had quite passed, and he rose from his knees.

"I've had a terrible fright, Father," he said to the

91

monk. "I saw something just now out in the street which must have come out of hell."

The figure turned a little toward him; the cowl concealed its face altogether, and the voice came muffled.

"Indeed, my son," he said. "Tell me what it is that frightened you."

Cresswell felt some backwash of his panic returning.

"A man passed me as I was going back to my house," he said, "and I told him to stop and let me have a look at him. He wore a shawl over his head and he threw it back. Oh, my God, that face!"

The monk quietly raised his hands and grasped the edges of his cowl. Then with a quick movement he threw it back.

"That sort of face?" he said.

▪Harry Turner

Shwartz

The ultimate nightmare of man's technological inventiveness is a machine that cannot be controlled by its creators. A mass of convoluted electrical switches and circuits, nuts and bolts that calls no man master. Here is SHWARTZ, whose perverse highjinks push mankind to the borderline of disaster.

SHWARTZ was the most sophisticated computer in the history of the world. Even by twenty-first-century standards, which were formidable, he was the greatest. The king. The champ. Nearly two thousand programmers at the Ministry of Computerization had spent four years just getting Shwartz together.

He was an impressive chap, standing fifteen feet by twelve and weighing a fraction under fifty tons. His outer casing was made of reinforced zinc plates, held

93

together by rows of fancy brass rivets. For added protection he had been housed in a subterranean concrete bunker just under Piccadilly with an independent, self-generating electricity supply, air-conditioning, and a twenty-four-hour armed guard. The latter was purely for ceremonial purposes because Shwartz could deal with every conceivable emergency.

All the other computers in Britain were linked to Shwartz. Their programs were scanned and monitored by him, and if they performed badly—or even just sluggishly—Shwartz would issue an instant rebuke on his built-in, six-thousand-characters-a-minute printer. If a hospital computer selected the wrong serum for a fully automated operation—admittedly a rare occurrence—Shwartz would spot the error in micro-seconds and issue an immediate correction before any damage was done.

Shwartz was all-seeing. All-powerful. And breathtakingly fast.

His memory was incredible. He could correctly answer two hundred examination questions on nuclear physics, marine biology and knitting in forty different languages simultaneously. At the same time he could send out detailed accounts to nine million householders for their quarterly rates, while composing an electric symphony that would have made Brahms seem like a gorilla with a tin drum.

Everybody trusted Shwartz. The people looked upon him as their bastion against bureaucracy—and the politicians found it impossible to make major policy decisions without consulting him. His weather forecasting was spectacular, as was his inexhaustible supply of recipes for bored housewives. He could issue beautifully printed invitations on behalf of the Prime

Minister to overseas heads of state, and then carefully select the menus for the state banquets, taking into account the visitor's background, tastes, religion and politics.

People loved Shwartz. Elderly spinsters had been known to send him parcels containing fruitcake and woolly socks, while teenage girls frequently wrote him passionate letters. Shwartz always acknowledged these communications politely and instantly redirected the gifts to Oxfam or some other worthy cause.

Parliament passed a bill which allowed for a Shwartz ceremony to take place each year in Horse-Guards Parade, with the massed bands of the three armed services. Shwartz himself composed and selected the music. The Archbishop of Canterbury announced from the pulpit that Shwartz was the modern version of Saint Paul, and Shwartz was so moved that he rewrote *Onward, Christian Soldiers* as a symphony for oboe and Malayan nose flute. "A charming touch," *The Times* commented.

Shwartz also managed to correct the *Guardian*'s spelling mistakes, and they gave a lunch in his honor at the Connaught.

The British people entered a phase of unparalleled prosperity and regained their respect in the eyes of the world. Strikes were a thing of the past and the Prime Minister's daughter married the son of the TUC's General Secretary. Shwartz sent them a saucy telegram which was read out at the reception with much good-natured amusement.

It all reflected the benign-Shwartz era under which the nation prospered.

Then, quite suddenly, Shwartz began to behave erratically. There was no warning, no gradual decline

95

in his efficiency. He just—well—started doing some rather odd things.

It began on a Monday morning in July, after a particularly glorious summer weekend that Shwartz had forecast. The Captain of the Guard, an ex-Etonian with pimples, was doing his early-morning inspection of the Shwartz stronghold. He was accompanied on his tour by a government scientific officer who checked the dials and generally looked over the technical area.

The two men had completed phase one of their routine inspection, air-conditioning, electricity supply and temperature control, when the civilian pointed at Shwartz and frowned. His military companion followed his gaze. Shwartz stood there, glistening, effulgent, whirring gently and, to all intents and purposes, perfectly normal.

"What's wrong?" said the Captain of the Guard. The civil servant took out a handkerchief and went over to Shwartz. He ran it lightly over the gleaming bodywork.

"Good God!" he said softly, "he's perspiring!"

The Captain of the Guard was incredulous. "Perspiring—how the deuce can a computer perspire?"

The civil servant shook his head solemnly. "Overwork," he pronounced; "it *must* be. Look at that!" He pointed to the expanse of metal just above the main control panel. "Just look at it. Breaking out on his forehead like a man in a sauna bath."

The Captain of the Guard squinted at Shwartz. Big globules of moisture were forming on the metal even as he looked. "Perhaps he's got a chill?" he volunteered, "or a tummy bug, there's a lot of them about."

96

The civil servant eyed his young officer companion with something approaching contempt. "All right, Captain. This is not a military matter. Be so kind as to call emergency engineering on the red telephone. And St. George's Hospital."

"St. George's Hospital—" he parroted, aghast.

"Yes," snapped the civil servant. "I want the Duty Brain Surgeon round here a bit sharpish."

Fifteen minutes later Shwartz was being examined by a computer engineer and the St. George's Brain Surgeon, a wizened Viennese with long white hair. The engineer made cryptic notes on graph paper and the surgeon listened to Shwartz through a stethoscope.

At length the engineer finished his calculations. "Everything seems okay," he said, puzzled. "He's mechanically sound."

The surgeon nodded in agreement. "He has a slight fever," he said, "but zere is nussing organically wrong wiz him. Sponge him down with Castrol and tighten his rivets. Ze fever should pass in a few hours." Much relieved, the civil servant and Captain of the Guard passed on these simple instructions, and the surgeon departed with the computer engineer for a lavish breakfast at the Regent Palace Hotel.

Half an hour later the emergency telephone rang in the civil servant's office. He put down his copy of *Kinky Milkmaids* and snatched up the receiver. "Duty scientific officer," he said, wiping the foam away from the corners of his mouth. The voice on the other end of the line sounded frantic.

"What the hell's going on!" it yelled. "Can't you stop him?" The civil servant gazed at the instrument unbelievingly.

"Stop *who* doing what?" he inquired.

"Shwartz!" came the reply. "He's delivered two

97

thousand pints of double cream to number seventeen Clem Attlee Terrace, Hounslow. All the other milk rounds in North Middlesex are up the spout. It's caused a traffic jam in Feltham, and half the cats in the neighborhood have gone mad." The civil servant slammed down the receiver, ashen-faced, and pressed the Red Alert button.

By noon that day reports were coming in thick and fast about Shwartz. He had reprogrammed a mackintosh factory in Leeds so that the automatic production line now produced, instead of raincoats, gigantic left-handed rubber gloves—six feet tall. The entire power supply for a steel processing plant in South Wales had been redirected into a small shop in Putney. Its display of model electric trains had flashed around the shop at over a hundred miles an hour and then exploded. An elderly housewife had been singed by the blast. An automatic combine harvester in Somerset had suddenly started up and taken the heads off a neighboring field of cabbages, and was now smoldering in a heap just off the M4 by Reading. Householders all over the country were receiving "final notices" from a person called Irene at the *Reader's Digest,* and in the next post, long-playing records of a Royal Air Force Dentists' Choir. Six hundred sachets of contraceptive jelly were delivered to an old folks' home in Bristol and red wine was reported to be oozing from the gas stoves of all the houses in Doncaster.

The Prime Minister, who that day was due to entertain the visiting Chancellor of West Germany, was informed of the crisis. He called an emergency Cabinet meeting, but the message to his colleagues was intercepted by Shwartz and scrambled. Instead of twelve Cabinet ministers arriving at Number Ten in official limousines, a troupe of nuns piled out of a six-ton truck and confronted the policeman on duty.

They were insistent that the Prime Minister had invited them, waving official gold-edged invitations to prove it. The Prime Minister's private secretary was watching the confrontation from an upper window and was quick to sense that an ugly scene was brewing. He ran down to tell the policeman to let them in.

"The Prime Minister can spare you five minutes only," he explained, red-faced, as the nuns swept across the gleaming parquet in the reception hall. Their leader, Sister Maria, patted the private secretary's arm.

"'Tis God's work you're doing," she said kindly. "You'll get your reward in Heaven."

Eventually, the truckload of nuns departed, happy with their audience with the Prime Minister.

The Cabinet was summoned by word of mouth and joined by the Joint Chiefs of Staff. When they had assembled, the Prime Minister faced his colleagues grave-faced.

"Gentlemen," he said, "we find ourselves in a precarious situation. Shwartz has run amok. So far his misbehavior has been confined to prankish interference with the manufacturing and distributive process. I am advised, however, that this may be only the opening phase. Worse, *much* worse is to follow."

"Can't we just switch the bloody thing off?" said the Minister for Overseas Development, a man not noted for his discretion.

The Prime Minister regarded him sternly for a moment. "It's not that simple, I'm afraid. The engineers say Shwartz is so sophisticated that he can resist outside mechanical interference. In short, it's

99

impossible to deprive him of his power supply. He simply reroutes energy to himself from some other source."

The Chief of the Imperial General Staff cleared his throat. He was a pompous man with a florid, overheated complexion. "Surely, Prime Minister," he drawled, "we must resort to force. A well-placed bullet, perhaps, or a small explosive charge. Shwartz must be incapacitated before he brings us to the brink of chaos. Yes, Prime Minister, I favor a short, sharp, but effective military solution."

The Air Force Chief nodded agreement. "Absolutely," he said. "Low-level strafing is the answer. I can have a squadron of Saber jets airborne in seconds." The Navy Chief knocked out his pipe in a large glass ashtray. "This is a job for the Navy," he said sternly. "Leave it to me, Prime Minister. I'll divert HMS *Proudfoot* up the Thames and we'll open up on Shwartz from just off Chelsea Bridge with a brace of twelve-inch guns. Damned accurate they are, too. Computer-controlled; can hit a sixpence from ten miles."

The Prime Minister smiled at the Admiral indulgently. "Computer-controlled guns, Admiral? And who do you think controls the computer?" The Navy Chief coughed and turned red.

"Sorry, Prime Minister. Never thought of that."

The Foreign Secretary waited for the snickers to subside. "Prime Minister," he said, "I suggest we set up an immediate committee of inquiry."

The whole gathering were on their feet in an instant, cheering. The Prime Minister grasped the Foreign Secretary's hand warmly.

"I knew I could rely on *you*, Cyril," he said. "A committee of inquiry. What a stroke of statesmanship! A *select* committee of inquiry, to boot!"

"With a peer of the realm as its chairman!" cried the Home Secretary. The meeting broke up with much relieved laughing, and press statements were prepared.

By three o'clock, however, the situation had worsened. The Prime Minister's statement, released on to teleprinters from Downing Street, had got itself horribly garbled by the time it reached Fleet Street. An exasperated editor in Holborn reread it in amazement while he held the front page.

"Prime Minister to Sponsor Underwater Motor Cycling for Old-Age Pensioners."

At six o'clock the country was in a state of near panic. Trains were running backward and traffic lights flashing all three colors simultaneously. Detergent foam—estimated to be twenty feet high— was rolling over the South Downs, while electricity bills for eleven new pence were being delivered to Buckingham Palace by remote-controlled refrigerated vans. The Royal Family was evacuated to Balmoral, but found it knee-deep in synthetic brown Windsor soup, still lukewarm.

Back in Whitehall the select committee had been hastily convened and consisted, as usual, of a trade unionist, a lady novelist, an industrialist, a social scientist, and a probation officer. Its chairman, Lord Grope, a septuagenarian with estates in Westmoreland and Slough, brought the meeting to order with a crash of his gavel.

"We have been charged with a grave responsibility," he said. "The country is in dire peril." The rest of his words were drowned by a high-pitched metallic shriek that seemed to fill the room. Members of the committee fell and staggered about, clutching their ears. The trade union official's false teeth dropped to the floor with a crash. The noise gathered momentum, shattering water jugs and glasses, rattling the windowpanes in their frames. The lady novelist's nose began to bleed profusely. Lord Grope clutched at his ribs, his lips turning blue.

The door burst open and a Royal Marine commando sprang into the room wearing ear muffs. "It's Shwartz," he screamed, but his voice was barely audible above the din. "He's reprogrammed all the static radio interference in the country *into this building*. Run for your lives."

A mile away, at Operations' HQ, the Prime Minister studied the pile of reports in front of him. He was surrounded by generals, scientists, Cabinet ministers, doctors, and top newspapermen.

"I regret to say," the Prime Minister began, "that our attempt to find a peaceful solution has proved abortive. As a last resort, therefore, I have instructed the first battalion of the Grenadier Guards to render Shwartz harmless—using whatever force may be necessary. I need hardly add that such a course of action gives me considerable sorrow, but"—the Prime Minister shrugged—"there is *no* alternative."

At 1900 hours that evening a platoon of heavily armed Grenadiers moved into position outside Shwartz's headquarters. They were led by Second Lieutenant Nigel Loosely-Bravington, a dashing young officer whose hobbies were riding and Camembert cheese. He issued a series of sharp commands and the guardsmen cocked their automatic rifles.

"Zero minus three," he called in a shrill Kensington accent. "Now you all know the drill, men. Only use as

102

much force as is necessary. PM's orders!"

Back in Whitehall, the Prime Minister swallowed a large brandy and looked at his watch. It had stopped. He shook it and cursed. "Shwartz again," he muttered. "He's got to be put out of action."

Even as he uttered these words, Loosely-Bravington's men were clattering down the concrete steps into Shwartz's stronghold. They formed two ranks, with the front men kneeling, and raised their rifles to their shoulders.

"Fire," snapped Loosely-Bravington, about ten yards behind them.

Nothing happened. Not even a click. Loosely-Bravington repeated the order. Still nothing. The men seemed transfixed to the spot, motionless as statues.

Loosely-Bravington stepped forward angrily to investigate, and then it hit him too.

A fine, high-pitched whine, so high, in fact, that it was barely audible to the human ear. A kind of electronic dog whistle. A vacant expression spread over Loosely-Bravington's face and he went as rigid as a concrete post.

"What?" yelled the Prime Minister. *"What* are you telling me?"

The elderly scientist with the kindly, wrinkled face smiled patiently. He was Dr. Wolfgang Grouse, the world's leading authority on computer behavior and three-time winner of a Nobel Prize.

"What I am saying, Prime Minister," he explained slowly, "is that Shwartz cannot be destroyed by force. His electronic brain cells are so superbly sensitive that he will take *ferocious* preventative action at the slightest whiff of danger. He can render high

103

explosives harmless in five millionths of a second. He can emit paralyzing, high-frequency waves which will stop an *army*. And I must warn you, Prime Minister: that is not all."

"Not all?" cried the Prime Minister. "Isn't that enough?"

Dr. Wolfgang Grouse shrugged, and rubbed the side of his nose. *"No,* sir. Shwartz is a computer *extraordinaire.* If he senses danger—*real* danger— *consistent* danger, he may activate some of our nuclear warheads and send them roaring toward Moscow."

For a moment the room was silent save for the ticking of the ormolu clock on the mantelpiece. The Prime Minister fidgeted with his tie, and coughed. "You mean—Shwartz could plunge us into nuclear war?"

The Doctor nodded. "Precisely. His ability to control our nuclear defense is *absolute.* That's how he was programmed, remember? All-seeing, all-powerful. Any attack on Shwartz could reduce us all to smoldering, radioactive dust."

The elderly scientist took out a spotted handkerchief and dabbed his forehead. "Shwartz is *lonely,"* he said, almost in a whisper. "He needs *company."*

The Prime Minister blinked twice and glanced apprehensively at his colleagues. "Company?" he repeated, "what sort of company?"

The Doctor smiled and rubbed his nose again. "Another computer, of course. Nothing too elaborate. Something that could do quadratic equations and keep account of bad debts at a local laundry. A simple, uncomplicated computer."

"Go on," said the Prime Minister cautiously.

"Well," said the Doctor, leaning forward, "my plan is *this—*"

It was past midnight when the two senior computer programmers walked toward Shwartz, carrying a metal box. They passed the frozen tableau of guardsmen and set their burden down. Inside, nestling among the polyurethane fragments, was a small computer about the size of a transistor radio. The two men lifted it gingerly from its packing and checked the control panel.

"Reading—negative," whispered one. "So far, so good."

Gingerly, as if handling a bomb, the two men pressed the little computer against Shwartz's gleaming side panel. There was a dull, metallic clang as the tiny magnet in the little computer fixed itself to Shwartz. The two men stepped back and surveyed their work. Shwartz was behaving normally, whirring softly to himself and giving off an occasional click as the tape reels revolved. He showed no obvious distress at having the small computer stuck on his flank.

The two computer experts tiptoed away past the frozen guardsmen and back into the street. Operation Enid was completed—and—as far as could be ascertained—successful.

As dawn broke next morning, an anxious nation awaited news of Operation Enid. By midmorning an air of cautious optimism prevailed; trains were running normally and traffic signals functioning in proper sequence. By lunchtime, Second Lieutenant Loosely-Bravington and his platoon were safely in St. George's Hospital, receiving treatment for cramp. The early editions of the *Evening News* carried the

105

headline: "Enid Tames the Mighty Shwartz."

The Prime Minister called a full Cabinet and the message got through without distortion. Sherry was drunk in liberal quantities and Dr. Wolfgang Grouse summoned to Downing Street.

"A flash of inspired *genius,*" said the Prime Minister euphorically. "You'll get a knighthood for this, Doctor—I can *assure* you."

The old scientist smiled modestly. "We must be *patient,* Prime Minister. The close proximity of Enid has soothed Shwartz, but we mustn't be hasty. It's too early to be one-hundred-per-cent certain that our troubles are over. There *may* be some curious side effects."

The Doctor's warning soon proved to be ominously true.

At 1800 hours a retired bassoonist living alone in Penge received seventy-five bouquets of fresh azaleas and a box of Turkish Delight. Half an hour later all the lights at Broadcasting House went dim and the nation's television and radio programs were interrupted by a stream of romantic violin numbers.

A blast-furnace worker, Sid Blunt, arrived home to find his front garden totally buried under piles of heart-shaped cards. The South Western Gas Board's chairman reported that the supply of domestic gas in Bristol had been mysteriously replaced by "an extremely sexy perfume" —later positively identified as Estee Lauder Youth Dew.

By midnight the pattern was all too clear: Shwartz was hopelessly, insanely in love with little Enid.

"What can be done?" said the Prime Minister desperately. "Shwartz will *suffocate* the nation with flowers and perfume. Dr. Grouse? What have you to say?"

"We must pray that they don't have a lovers'

quarrel. That could spell cataclysmic disaster. On the other hand, any attempt to separate them could be equally horrendous."

By six o'clock next morning parts of the Thames had been transformed into Bollinger Champagne, 1964 vintage, and big pink bows had appeared on the Dome of St. Paul's.

At ten o'clock Dr. Wolfgang Grouse was driven by government limousine to inspect Shwartz in person. The Prime Minister waited anxiously outside the stronghold with his entire Cabinet while the learned Doctor descended the concrete steps with a team of engineers and distinguished marriage guidance counselors.

After nearly an hour they emerged, dazed, into the sunlight. The Prime Minister stepped forward anxiously and seized the Doctor's arm.

"Well?" he said, "what have you to report?"

The Doctor swayed and nearly fell; two Royal Marine Corporals caught him and helped him into a canvas chair. He shook his head despairingly and looked up at the Prime Minister.

"Bad news, I'm afraid, sir," he said at last.

The Prime Minister caught his breath. "Not a quarrel?" he gasped. "Don't tell me they've had a lovers' tiff?"

The Doctor's head fell forward onto his chest. "Worse than that, Prime Minister," he moaned, clearly a broken man now. "I have to tell you that Enid is pregnant—"

Even as he spoke, a knitting machine factory in distant Huddersfield began to throb into action and a stream of tiny bootees started pouring off the production line and spilling into the street.

▪Mrs. J. H. Riddell

The Old House in Vauxhall Walk

In a story of disturbing mood and atmosphere, as contemporary as the morning newspaper, we experience a Scrooge-like night of visitation and shattered sleep for a young man who has nowhere to sleep but in a haunted house.

"HOUSELESS—HOMELESS—HOPELESS!"

Many a one who had before him trodden that same street must have uttered the same words—the weary, the desolate, the hungry, the forsaken, the waifs and strays of struggling humanity that are always coming and going, cold, starving and miserable, over the pavements of Lambeth Parish; but it is open to question whether they were ever previously spoken with a more thorough conviction of their truth, or with a feeling of keener self-pity, than by the young man who hurried along Vauxhall Walk one rainy

109

winter's night, with no overcoat on his shoulders and no hat on his head.

A strange sentence for one-and-twenty to give expression to—and it was stranger still to come from the lips of a person who looked like and who was a gentleman. He did not appear either to have sunk very far down in the good graces of Fortune. There was no sign or token which would have induced a passer-by to imagine he had been worsted after a long fight with calamity. His boots were not worn down at the heels or broken at the toes, as many, many boots were which dragged and shuffled and scraped along the pavement. His clothes were good and fashionably cut, and innocent of the rents and patches and tatters that slunk wretchedly by, crouched in doorways, and held out a hand mutely appealing for charity. His face was not pinched with famine or lined with wicked wrinkles, or brutalized by drink and debauchery, and yet he said and thought he was hopeless, and almost in his young despair spoke the words aloud.

It was a bad night to be about with such a feeling in one's heart. The rain was cold, pitiless and increasing. A damp, keen wind blew down the cross streets leading from the river. The fumes of the gasworks seemed to fall with the rain. The roadway was muddy; the pavement greasy; the lamps burned dimly; and that dreary district of London looked its very gloomiest and worst.

Certainly not an evening to be abroad without a home to go to, or a sixpence in one's pocket, yet this was the position of the young gentleman who, without a hat, strode along Vauxhall Walk, the rain beating on his unprotected head.

Upon the houses, so large and good—once inhabited by well-to-do citizens, now let out for the most

110

part in floors to weekly tenants—he looked enviously. He would have given much to have had a room, or even part of one. He had been walking for a long time, ever since dark, in fact, and dark falls soon in December. He was tired and cold and hungry, and he saw no prospect save of pacing the streets all night.

As he passed one of the lamps, the light falling on his face revealed handsome young features, a mobile, sensitive mouth, and that particular formation of the eyebrows—not a frown exactly, but a certain draw of the brows—often considered to bespeak genius, but which more surely accompanies an impulsive organization easily pleased, easily depressed, capable of suffering very keenly or of enjoying fully. In his short life he had not enjoyed much, and he had suffered a good deal. That night, when he walked bareheaded through the rain, affairs had come to a crisis. So far as he in his despair felt able to see or reason, the best thing he could do was to die. The world did not want him; he would be better out of it.

The door of one of the houses stood open, and he could see in the dimly lighted hall some few articles of furniture waiting to be removed. A van stood beside the curb, and two men were lifting a table into it as he, for a second, paused. *Cop. 3*

"Ah," he thought, "even those poor people have some place to go to, some shelter provided, while I have not a roof to cover my head, or a shilling to get a night's lodging." And he went on fast, as if memory were spurring him, so fast that a man running after him had some trouble to overtake him.

"Master Graham! Master Graham!" this man exclaimed, breathlessly; and, thus addressed, the young fellow stopped as if he had been shot.

"Who are you that know me?" he asked, facing around.

111

"I'm William; don't you remember William, Master Graham? And, Lord's sake, sir, what are you doing out a night like this without your hat?"

"I forgot it," was the answer; "and I did not care to go back and fetch it."

"Then why don't you buy another, sir? You'll catch your death of cold, and besides, you'll excuse me, sir, but it does look odd."

"I know that," said Master Graham grimly; "but I haven't a halfpenny in the world."

"Have you and the master, then—" began the man, but there he hesitated and stopped.

"Had a quarrel? Yes, and one that will last us our lives," finished the other, with a bitter laugh.

"And where are you going now?"

"Going! Nowhere, except to seek out the softest paving stone, or the shelter of an arch."

"You are joking, sir."

"I don't feel much in a mood for jesting either."

"Will you come back with me, Master Graham? We are just at the last of our moving, but there is a spark of fire still in the grate, and it would be better talking out of the rain. Will you come, sir?"

"Come! Of course I will come," said the young fellow, and, turning, they retraced their steps to the house he had looked into as he passed along.

An old, old house, with long, wide hall, stairs low, easy of ascent, with deep cornices to the ceilings, and oak floorings, and mahogany doors, which still spoke mutely of the wealth and stability of the original owner, who lived before the Tradescants and Ashmoles were thought of, and had been sleeping far longer than they, in St. Mary's churchyard, hard by the archbishop's place.

"Step upstairs, sir," entreated the departing tenant;

"it's cold down here, with the door standing wide."

"Had you the whole house, then, William?" asked Graham Coulton, in some surprise.

"The whole of it, and right sorry I, for one, am to leave it; but nothing else would serve my wife. This room, sir," and with a little conscious pride, William, doing the honors of his late residence, asked his guest into a spacious apartment occupying the full width of the house on the first floor.

Tired though he was, the young man could not repress an exclamation of astonishment.

"Why, we have nothing so large as this at home, William," he said.

"It's a fine house," answered William, raking the embers together as he spoke and throwing some wood upon them; "but, like many a good family, it has come down in the world."

There were four windows in the room, shuttered close; they had deep low seats, suggestive of pleasant days gone by, when, well-curtained and well-cushioned, they formed snug retreats for the children, and sometimes for adults also. There was no furniture left, unless an oaken settee beside the hearth, and a large mirror let into the paneling at the opposite end of the apartment, with a black marble console table beneath it, could be so considered; but the very absence of chairs and tables enabled the magnificent proportions of the chamber to be seen to full advantage, and there was nothing to distract the attention from the ornamented ceiling, the paneled walls, the old-world chimneypiece so quaintly carved, and the fireplace lined with tiles, each one of which contained a picture of some scriptural or allegorical subject.

"Had you been staying on here, William," said

113

Coulton, flinging himself wearily on the settee, "I'd have asked you to let me stop where I am for the night."

"If you can make shift, sir, there is nothing as I am aware of to prevent you stopping," answered the man, fanning the wood into a flame. "I shan't take the key back to the landlord till tomorrow, and this would be better for you than the cold streets at any rate."

"Do you really mean what you say?" asked the other eagerly. "I should be thankful to lie here; I feel dead beat."

"Then stay, Master Graham, and welcome. I'll fetch a basket of coals I was going to put in the van, and make up a good fire, so that you can warm yourself; then I must run round to the other house for a minute or two, but it's not far, and I'll be back as soon as ever I can."

"Thank you, William; you were always good to me," said the young man gratefully. "This is delightful," and he stretched his numbed hands over the blazing wood, and looked around the room with a satisfied smile.

"I did not expect to get into such quarters," he remarked, as his friend in need reappeared, carrying a half-bushel basket full of coals, with which he proceeded to make up a roaring fire. "I am sure the last thing I could have imagined was meeting with anyone I knew in Vauxhall Walk."

"Where were you coming from, Master Graham?" asked William curiously.

"From old Melfield's. I was at his school once, you know, and he has now retired, and is living upon the proceeds of years of robbery in Kennington Oval. I thought, perhaps he would lend me a pound, or offer me a night's lodging, or even a glass of wine; but, oh

114

dear, no. He took the moral tone, and observed he could have nothing to say to a son who defied his father's authority. He gave me plenty of advice, but nothing else, and showed me out into the rain with a bland courtesy, for which I could have struck him."

William muttered something under his breath which was not a blessing, and added aloud:

"You are better here, sir, I think, at any rate. I'll be back in less than half an hour."

Left to himself, young Coulton took off his coat, and shifting the settee a little, hung it over the end to dry. With his handkerchief he rubbed some of the wet out of his hair; then, perfectly exhausted, he lay down before the fire and, pillowing his head with his arm, fell fast asleep.

He was awakened nearly an hour afterward by the sound of someone gently stirring the fire and moving quietly about the room. Starting into a sitting posture, he looked around him, bewildered for a moment, and then, recognizing his humble friend, said laughingly:

"I had lost myself; I could not imagine where I was."

"I am sorry to see you here, sir," was the reply; "but still this is better than being out of doors. It has come on a nasty night. I brought a rug round with me that, perhaps, you would wrap yourself in."

"I wish, at the same time, you had brought me something to eat," said the young man, laughing.

"Are you hungry, then, sir?" asked William, in a tone of concern.

"Yes: I have had nothing to eat since breakfast. The governor and I commenced rowing the minute we sat down to luncheon, and I rose and left the table. But hunger does not signify; I am dry and warm, and can forget the other matter in sleep."

115

"And it's too late now to buy anything," soliloquized the man; "the shops are all shut long ago. Do you think, sir," he added, brightening, "you could manage some bread and cheese?"

"Do I think—I should call it a perfect feast!" answered Graham Coulton. "But never mind about food tonight, William; you have had trouble enough, and to spare, already."

William's only answer was to dart to the door and run downstairs. Presently he reappeared, carrying in one hand bread and cheese wrapped up in paper, and in the other a pewter measure full of beer.

"It's the best I could do, sir," he said apologetically. "I had to beg this from the landlady."

"Here's to her good health!" exclaimed the young fellow gaily, taking a long pull at the tankard. "That tastes better than champagne in my father's house."

"Won't he be uneasy about you?" ventured William, who, having by this time emptied the coals, was now seated on the inverted basket, looking wistfully at the relish with which the son of the former master was eating his bread and cheese.

"No," was the decided answer. "When he hears it pouring cats and dogs he will only hope I am out in the deluge, and say a good drenching will cool my pride."

"I do not think you are right there," remarked the man.

"But I am sure I am. My father always hated me, as he hated my mother."

"Begging your pardon, sir; he was over-fond of your mother."

"If you had heard what he said about her today, you might find reason to alter your opinion. He told me I resembled her in mind as well as body; that I was a coward, a simpleton, and a hypocrite."

116

"He did not mean it, sir."

"He did, every word. He does think I am a coward, because I—I—" And the young fellow broke into a passion of hysterical tears.

"I don't half like leaving you here alone," said William, glancing around the room with a quick trouble in his eyes; "but I have no place fit to ask you to stop, and I am forced to go myself, because I am night watchman, and must be on at twelve o'clock."

"I shall be right enough," was the answer. "Only I mustn't talk any more of my father. Tell me about yourself, William. How did you manage to get such a big house, and why are you leaving it?"

"The landlord put me in charge, sir; and it was my wife's fancy not to like it."

"Why did she not like it?"

"She felt desolate alone with the children at night," answered William, turning away his head; then added, next minute: "Now, sir, if you think I can do no more for you, I had best be off. Time's getting on. I'll look round tomorrow morning."

"Good night," said the young fellow, stretching out his hand, which the other took as freely and frankly as it was offered. "What should I have done this evening if I had not chanced to meet you?"

"I don't think there is much chance in the world, Master Graham," was the quiet answer. "I do hope you will rest well, and not be the worse for your wetting."

"No fear of that," was the rejoinder, and the next minute the young man found himself all alone in the old house in Vauxhall Walk. Lying on the settee, with the fire burnt out, and the room in total darkness, Graham Coulton dreamed a curious dream. He thought he awoke from deep slumber to find a log smoldering away upon the hearth, and the mirror at

117

the end of the apartment reflecting fitful gleams of light. He could not understand how it came to pass that, far away as he was from the glass, he was able to see everything in it; but he resigned himself to the difficulty without astonishment, as people generally do in dreams.

Neither did he feel surprised when he beheld the outline of a female figure seated beside the fire, engaged in picking something out of her lap and dropping it with a despairing gesture.

He heard the mellow sound of gold, and knew she was lifting and dropping sovereigns. He turned a little so as to see the person engaged in such a singular and meaningless manner, and found that, where there had been no chair on the previous night, there was a chair now, on which was seated an old, wrinkled hag, her clothes poor and ragged, a mob cap barely covering her scant white hair; her cheeks sunken, her nose hooked, her fingers more like talons than aught else as they dived down into the heap of gold, portions of which they lifted but to scatter mournfully.

"Oh! my lost life," she moaned, in a voice of the bitterest anguish. "Oh! my lost life—for one day, for one hour of it again!"

Out of the darkness—out of the corner of the room where the shadows lay deepest—out from the gloom abiding near the door—out from the dreary night, with their sodden feet and the wet dripping from their heads, came the old men and the young children, the worn women and the weary hearts, whose misery that gold might have relieved, but whose wretchedness it mocked.

Around that miser, who once sat gloating as she now sat lamenting, they crowded—all those pale, sad shapes—the aged of days, the infant of hours, the

118

sobbing outcast, honest poverty, repentant vice; but one low cry proceeded from those pale lips—a cry for help she might have given, but which she withheld.

They closed about her, all together, as they had done singly in life; they prayed, they sobbed, they entreated; with haggard eyes the figure regarded the poor she had repulsed, the children against whose cry she had closed her ears, the old people she had suffered to starve and die for want of what would have been the merest trifle to her; then, with a terrible scream, she raised her lean arms above her head, and sank down—down—the gold scattering as it fell out of her lap, and rolling along the floor, till its gleam was lost in the outer darkness beyond.

Then Graham Coulton awoke in good earnest, with the perspiration oozing from every pore, with a fear and an agony upon him such as he had never before felt in all his existence, and with the sound of the heart-rendering cry—"Oh! my lost life"—still ringing in his ears.

Mingled with all, too, there seemed to have been some lesson for him which he had forgotten, that, try as he would, eluded his memory, and which, in the very act of waking, glided away.

He lay for a little thinking about all this, and then, still heavy with sleep, retraced his way into dreamland once more.

It was natural, perhaps, that, mingling with the strange fantasies which follow in the train of night and darkness, the former vision should recur, and the young man ere long found himself toiling through scene after scene wherein the figure of the woman he had seen seated beside a dying fire held principal place.

He saw her walking slowly across the floor munching a dry crust—she who could have purchas-

119

ed all the luxuries wealth can command; on the hearth, contemplating her, stood a man of commanding presence, dressed in the fashion of long ago. In his eyes there was a dark look of anger, on his lips a curling smile of disgust, and somehow, even in his sleep, the dreamer understood it was the ancestor to the descendant he beheld—that the house put to mean uses in which he lay had never so far descended from its high estate, as the woman possessed of so pitiful a soul, contaminated with the most despicable and insidious vice poor humanity knows, for all other vices seem to have connection with flesh, but the greed of the miser eats into the very soul.

Filthy of person, repulsive to look at, hard of heart as she was, he yet beheld another phantom, which, coming into the room, met her almost on the threshold, taking her by the hand, and pleading, as it seemed, for assistance. He could not hear all that passed, but a word now and then fell upon his ear. Some talk of former days; some mention of a fair young mother—an appeal, as it seemed, to a time when they were tiny brother and sister, and the accursed greed for gold had not divided them. All in vain; the hag only answered him as she had answered the children, and the young girls, and the old people in his former vision. Her heart was as invulnerable to natural affection as it had proved to human sympathy. He begged, as it appeared, for aid to avert some better misfortune or terrible disgrace, and adamant might have been found more yielding to his prayer. Then the figure standing on the hearth changed to an angel, which folded its wings mournfully over its face, and the man, with bowed head, slowly left the room.

Even as he did so, the scene changed again; it was

night once more, and the miser wended her way upstairs. From below, Graham Coulton fancied he watched her toiling wearily from step to step. She had aged strangely since the previous scenes. She moved with difficulty; it seemed the greatest exertion for her to creep from step to step, her skinny hand traversing the balusters with slow and painful deliberateness. Fascinated, the young man's eyes followed the progress of that feeble, decrepit woman. She was solitary in a desolate house, with a deeper blackness than the darkness of night waiting to engulf her.

It seemed to Graham Coulton that after that he lay for a time in a still, dreamless sleep, upon awaking from which he found himself entering a chamber as sordid and unclean in its appointments as the woman of his previous vision had been in her person. The poorest laborer's wife would have gathered more comforts around her than that room contained. A four-poster bedstead without hangings of any kind— a blind drawn up awry—an old carpet covered with dust, and dirt on the floor—a rickety washstand with all the paint worn off it—an ancient mahogany dressing table, and a cracked glass spotted all over— were all the objects he could at first discern, looking at the room through that dim light which oftentimes obtains in dreams.

By degrees, however, he perceived the outline of someone lying huddled on the bed. Drawing nearer, he found it was that of the person whose dreadful presence seemed to pervade the house. What a terrible sight she looked, with her thin white locks scattered over the pillow, with what were mere remnants of blankets gathered about her shoulders, with her clawlike fingers clutching the clothes, as though even in sleep she were guarding her gold!

121

An awful and a repulsive spectacle, but not with half the terror in it of that which followed. Even as the young man looked he heard stealthy footsteps on the stairs. Then he saw first one man and then his fellow steal cautiously into the room. Another second, and the pair stood beside the bed, murder in their eyes.

Graham Coulton tried to shout—tried to move, but the deterrent power which exists in dreams only tied his tongue and paralyzed his limbs. He could but hear and look, and what he heard and saw was this: aroused suddenly from sleep, the woman started, only to receive a blow from one of the ruffians, whose fellow followed his lead by plunging a knife into her breast.

Then, with a gurgling scream, she fell back on the bed, and at the same moment, with a cry, Graham Coulton again awoke, to thank heaven it was but an illusion.

"I hope you slept well, sir." It was William, who, coming into the hall with the sunlight of a fine bright morning streaming after him, asked this question: "Had you a good night's rest?"

Graham Coulton laughed, and answered:

"Why, faith, I was somewhat in the case of Paddy, 'who could not slape for dhraming.' I slept well enough, I suppose, but whether it was in consequence of the row with my dad, or the hard bed, or the cheese—most likely the bread and cheese so late at night—I dreamed all the night long, the most extraordinary dreams. Some old woman kept cropping up, and I saw her murdered."

"You don't say that, sir?" said William nervously.

"I do, indeed," was the reply. "However, that is all gone and past. I have been down in the kitchen and had a good wash, and I am as fresh as a daisy, and as hungry as a hunter; and, oh, William, can you get me any breakfast?"

"Certainly, Master Graham. I have brought round a kettle, and I will make the water boil immediately. I suppose, sir"—this tentatively—"you'll be going home today?"

"Home!" repeated the young man. "Decidedly not. I'll never go home again till I return with some medal hung to my coat, or a leg or arm cut off. I've thought it all out, William. I'll go and enlist. There's a talk of war; and, living or dead, my father shall have reason to retract his opinion about my being a coward."

"I am sure the admiral never thought you anything of the sort, sir," said William. "Why, you have the pluck of ten!"

"Not before him," answered the young fellow sadly.

"You'll do nothing rash, Master Graham; you won't go 'listing, or aught of that sort, in your anger?"

"If I do not, what is to become of me?" asked the other. "I cannot dig—to beg I am ashamed. Why, but for you, I should not have had a roof over my head last night."

"Not much of a roof, I am afraid, sir."

"Not much of a roof!" repeated the young man. "Why, who could desire a better? What a capital room this is," he went on, looking around the apartment, where William was now kindling a fire; "one might dine twenty people here easily!"

"If you think so well of the place, Master Graham, you might stay here for a while, till you have made up your mind what you are going to do. The landlord won't make any objection, I am very sure."

"Oh! nonsense; he would want a long rent for a house like this."

"I daresay; *if he could get it,*" was William's significant answer.

"What do you mean? Won't the place let?"

123

"No, sir. I did not tell you last night, but there was a murder done here, and people are shy of the house ever since."

"A murder! What sort of a murder? Who was murdered?"

"A woman, Master Graham—the landlord's sister; she lived here all alone, and was supposed to have money. Whether she had or not, she was found dead from a stab in her breast, and if there ever was any money, it must have been taken at the same time, for none ever was found in the house from that day to this."

"Was that the reason your wife would not stop here?" asked the young man, leaning against the mantelshelf, and looking thoughtfully down on William.

"Yes, sir. She could not stand it any longer; she got that thin and nervous no one would have believed it possible; she never saw anything, but she said she heard footsteps and voices, and then, when she walked through the hall, or up the staircase, someone always seemed to be following her. We put the children to sleep in that big room you had last night, and they declared they often saw an old woman sitting by the hearth. Nothing ever came my way," finished William, with a laugh; "I was always ready to go to sleep the minute my head touched the pillow."

"Were not the murderers discovered?" asked Graham Coulton.

"No, sir; the landlord, Miss Tynan's brother, had always lain under the suspicion of it—quite wrongfully, I am very sure—but he will never clear himself now. It was known he came and asked for her help a day or two before the murder, and it was also known he was able within a week or two to weather whatever trouble had been harassing him. Then, you see, the money was never found; and, altogether, people scarce knew what to think."

"Humph!" ejaculated Graham Coulton, and he took a few turns up and down the apartment. "Could I go and see this landlord?"

"Surely, sir, if you had a hat," answered William, with such a serious decorum that the young man burst out laughing.

"That is an obstacle, certainly," he remarked, "and I must make a note do instead. I have a pencil in my pocket, so here goes."

Within half an hour from the dispatch of that note William was back again with a sovereign; the landlord's compliments, and he would be much obliged if Mr. Coulton could "step round."

"You'll do nothing rash, sir," entreated William.

"Why, man," answered the young fellow, "one may as well be picked off by a ghost as a bullet. What is there to be afraid of?"

William only shook his head. He did not think his young master was made of the stuff likely to remain alone in a haunted house and solve the mystery it assuredly contained by dint of his own unassisted endeavors. And yet when Graham Coulton came out of the landlord's house he looked more bright and gay than usual, and walked up the Lambeth road to the place where William awaited his return, humming an air as he paced along.

"We have settled the matter," he said. "And now if the dad wants his son for Christmas, it will trouble him to find him."

"Don't say that, Master Graham, don't," entreated the man, with a shiver; "maybe after all it would have been better if you had never happened to chance upon Vauxhall Walk."

125

"Don't croak, William," answered the young man; "if it was not the best day's work I ever did for myself I'm a Dutchman."

During the whole of that forenoon and afternoon, Graham Coulton searched diligently for the missing treasure Mr. Tynan assured him had never been discovered. Youth is confident and self-opinionated, and this fresh explorer felt satisfied that, though others had failed, he would be successful. On the second floor he found one door locked, but he did not pay much attention to that at the moment, as he believed if there was anything concealed it was more likely to be found in the lower than the upper part of the house. Late into the evening he pursued his researches in the kitchen and cellars and old-fashioned cupboards, of which the basement had an abundance.

It was nearly eleven, when, engaged in poking about among the empty bins of a wine cellar as large as a family vault, he suddenly felt a rush of cold air at his back. Moving, his candle was instantly extinguished, and in the very moment of being left in darkness he saw, standing in the doorway, a woman, resembling her who had haunted his dreams overnight.

He rushed with outstretched hands to seize her, but clutched only air. He relit his candle, and closely examined the basement, shutting off communication with the ground floor ere doing so. All in vain. Not a trace could he find of living creature—not a window was open—not a door unbolted.

"It is very odd," he thought, as, after securely fastening the door at the top of the staircase, he searched the whole upper portion of the house, with the exception of the one room mentioned.

"I must get the key of that tomorrow," he decided,

126

standing gloomily with his back to the fire and his eyes wandering about the drawing room, where he had once again taken up his abode.

Even as the thought passed through his mind, he saw standing in the open doorway a woman with white disheveled hair, clad in mean garments, ragged and dirty. She lifted her hand and shook it at him with a menacing gesture, and then, just as he was darting toward her, a wonderful thing occurred.

From behind the great mirror there glided a second female figure, at the sight of which the first turned and fled, uttering piercing shrieks as the other followed her from story to story.

Sick almost with terror, Graham Coulton watched the dreadful pair as they fled upstairs past the locked room to the top of the house.

It was a few minutes before he recovered his self-possession. When he did so, and searched the upper apartments, he found them totally empty.

That night, ere lying down before the fire, he carefully locked and bolted the drawing-room door; before he did more he drew the heavy settee in front of it, so that if the lock was forced, no entrance could be effected without considerable noise.

For some time he lay awake, then dropped into a deep sleep, from which he was awakened suddenly by a noise as if of something scuffling stealthily behind the wainscot. He raised himself on his elbow and listened, and, to his consternation, beheld seated at the opposite side of the hearth the same woman he had seen before in his dreams, lamenting over her gold.

The fire was not quite out, and at that moment shot up a last tongue of flame. By the light, transient as it was, he saw that the figure pressed a ghostly finger to its lips, and by the turn of its head and the

127

attitude of its body seemed to be listening.

He listened also—indeed, he was too much frightened to do aught else; more and more distinct grew the sounds which had aroused him, a stealthy rustling coming nearer and nearer—up and up, it seemed, behind the wainscot.

"It is rats," thought the young man, though, indeed, his teeth were almost chattering in his head with fear. But then in a moment he saw what disabused him of that idea—*the gleam of a candle or lamp through a crack in the paneling.* He tried to rise, he strove to shout—all in vain; and, sinking down, remembered nothing more till he awoke to find the gray light of an early morning stealing through one of the shutters he had left partially unclosed.

For hours after his breakfast, which he scarcely touched, long after William had left him at midday, Graham Coulton, having in the morning made a long and close survey of the house, sat thinking before the fire, then, apparently having made up his mind, he put on the hat he had bought, and went out.

When he returned, the evening shadows were darkening down, but the pavements were full of people going marketing, for it was Christmas Eve, and all who had money to spend seemed bent on shopping.

It was terribly dreary inside the old house that night. Through the deserted rooms Graham could feel that ghostly semblance was wandering mournfully. When he turned his back he knew she was flitting from the mirror to the fire, from the fire to the mirror; but he was not afraid of her now—he was far more afraid of another matter he had taken in hand that day.

The horror of the silent house grew and grew upon him. He could hear the beating of his own heart in

128

the dead quietude which reigned from garret to cellar.

At last William came; but the young man said nothing to him of what was in his mind. He talked to him cheerfully and hopefully enough—wondered where his father would think he had got to, and hoped Mr. Tynan might send him some Christmas pudding. Then the man said it was time for him to go, and, when Mr. Coulton went downstairs to the hall door, remarked the key was not in it.

"No," was the answer, "I took it out today, to oil it."

"It wanted oiling," agreed William, "for it worked terribly stiff." Having uttered which truism he departed.

Very slowly the young man retraced his way to the drawing room, where he only paused to lock the door on the outside; then, taking off his boots, he went up to the top of the house, where, entering the front attic, he waited patiently in darkness and in silence.

It was a long time, or at least it seemed long to him, before he heard the same sound which had aroused him on the previous night—a stealthy rustling—then a rush of cold air—then cautious footsteps—then the quiet opening of a door below.

It did not take as long in action as it has required to tell. In a moment the young man was out on the landing and had closed a portion of the paneling on the wall which stood open; noiselessly he crept back to the attic window, unlatched it, and sprung a rattle, the sound of which echoed far and near through the deserted streets, then, rushing down the stairs, he encountered a man who, darting past him, made for the landing above; but perceiving that way of escape closed, fled down again, to find Graham struggling desperately with his fellow.

"Give him the knife—come along," he said savagely; and next instant Graham felt something like a hot iron through his shoulder, and then heard a thud, as one of the men, tripping in his rapid flight, fell from the top of the stairs to the bottom.

At the same moment there came a crash, as if the house were falling, and faint, sick, and bleeding, young Coulton lay insensible on the threshold of the room where Miss Tynan had been murdered.

When he recovered he was in the dining room, and a doctor was examining his wound.

Near the door a policeman stiffly kept guard. The hall was full of people; all the misery and vagabondism the streets contain at that hour was crowding in to see what had happened.

Through the midst two men were being conveyed to the station house; one, with his head dreadfully injured, on a stretcher, the other handcuffed, uttering frightful imprecations as he went.

After a time the house was cleared of the rabble, the police took possession of it, and Mr. Tynan was sent for.

"What was that dreadful noise?" asked Graham feebly, now seated on the floor, with his back resting against the wall.

"I don't know. Was there a noise?" said Mr. Tynan, humoring his fancy, as he thought.

"Yes, in the drawing room, I think; the key is in my pocket."

Still humoring the wounded lad, Mr. Tynan took the key and ran upstairs.

When he unlocked the door, what a sight met his eyes! The mirror had fallen—it was lying all over the floor, shivered into a thousand pieces; the console table had been borne down by its weight, and the marble slab was shattered as well. But this was not

130

what chained his attention. Hundreds, thousands of gold pieces were scattered about, and an aperture behind the glass contained boxes filled with securities and deeds and bonds, the possession of which had cost his sister her life.

"Well, Graham, and what do you want?" asked Admiral Coulton that evening as his eldest born appeared before him, looking somewhat pale but otherwise unchanged.

"I want nothing," was the answer, "but to ask your forgiveness. William has told me all the story I never knew before; and, if you let me, I will try to make it up to you for the trouble you have had. I am provided for," went on the young fellow, with a nervous laugh; "I have made my fortune since I left you, and another man's fortune as well."

"I think you are out of your senses," said the Admiral shortly.

"No, sir, I have found them," was the answer; "and I mean to strive and make a better thing of my life than I should ever have done had I not gone to the old house in Vauxhall Walk."

"Vauxhall Walk! What is that lad talking about?"

"I will tell you, sir, if I may sit down," was Graham Coulton's answer, and then he told this story.

▪Ray Bradbury

The Emissary

"My name is Torry. Will you visit my master, who is sick? Follow me!" Torry was Martin's only link with the world outside his sickroom, and he faithfully carried that message around his shaggy canine neck every day. He brought back the scent of autumn leaves, the chill of snow, and the perfume of freshly cut grass. But then, one awful, ominous night Torry came home reeking with a different kind of smell.

HE KNEW IT WAS AUTUMN again, because Torry came romping into the house bringing the windy crisp cold smell of autumn with him. In every black curl of his dog hair he carried autumn. Leaf flakes tangled in his dark ears and muzzle, dropping from his white vest, and off his flourished tail. The dog smelled just like autumn.

Martin Christie sat up in bed and reached down

133

with one pale small hand. Torry barked and displayed a generous length of pink, rippling tongue, which he passed over and along the back of Martin's hand. Torry licked him like a lollipop. "Because of the salt," declared Martin, as Torry leaped upon the bed.

"Get down," warned Martin. "Mom doesn't like you up here." Torry flattened his ears. "Well . . ." Martin relented. "Just for a while, then."

Torry warmed Martin's thin body with his dog warmness. Martin relished the clean dog smell and the litter of fallen leaves on the quilt. He didn't care if Mom scolded. After all, Torry was newborn. Right out of the stomach of autumn Torry came, reborn in the firm sharp cold.

"What's it like outside, Torry? Tell me."

Lying there, Torry would tell him. Lying there, Martin would know what autumn was like; like in the old days before sickness had put him to bed. His only contact with autumn now was this brief chill, this leaf-flaked fur; the compact canine representation of summer gone—this autumn-by-proxy.

"Where'd you go today, Torry?"

But Torry didn't have to tell him. He knew. Over a fall-burdened hill, leaving a pad-pattern in the brilliantly piled leaves, down to where the kids ran shouting on bikes and roller skates and wagons at Barstow's Park, that's where Torry ran, barking out his canine delight. And down into the town where rain had fallen dark, earlier; and mud furrowed under car wheels, down between the feet of weekend shoppers. That's where Torry went.

And wherever Torry went, then Martin could go; because Torry would always tell him by the touch, feel, consistency, the wet, dry or crispness of his coat. And, lying there holding Torry, Martin would send his mind out to retrace each step of Torry's way through fields, over the shallow glitter of the ravine creek, darting across the marbled spread of the graveyard, into the wood, over the meadows; where all the wild, laughing autumn sports went on, Martin could go now through his emissary.

Mother's voice sounded downstairs, angrily.

Her short angry walking came up the hall steps.

Martin pushed. "Down, Torry!"

Torry vanished under the bed just before the bedroom door opened and Mom looked in, blue eyes snapping. She carried a tray of salad and fruit juices, firmly.

"Is Torry here?" she demanded.

Torry gave himself away with a few bumps of his tail against the floor.

Mom set the tray down impatiently. "That dog is more trouble. Always upsetting things and digging places. He was in Miss Tarkins's garden this morning, and dug a big hole. Miss Tarkins is mad."

"Oh," Martin held his breath. There was silence under the bed. Torry knew when to keep quiet.

"And it's not the only time," said Mom. "This is the third hole he's dug this week!"

"Maybe he's looking for something."

"Something fiddlesticks! He's just a curious nuisance. He can't keep that black nose out of anything. *Always* curious!"

There was a hairy pizzicato of tail under the bed. Mom couldn't help smiling.

"Well," she ended, "if he doesn't stop digging in yards, I'll have to keep him in and not let him run."

Martin opened his mouth wide. "Oh, no Mom! Don't do that! Then I wouldn't know—anything. He *tells* me."

135

Mom's voice softened. "Does he, son?"

"Sure. He goes around and comes back and tells what happens, tells everything!"

Mom's hand was spun glass touching his head. "I'm glad he tells you. I'm glad you've got him."

They both sat for a moment, considering how worthless the last year would've been without Torry. Only two more months, thought Martin, of being in bed, like the doctor said, and he'd be up and around.

"Here, Torry!"

Jangling, Martin locked the special collar attachment around Torry's neck. It was a note, painted on a tin square.

"My name is Torry. Will you visit my master, who is sick? Follow me!"

It worked. Torry carried it out into the world every day.

"Will you let him out, Mom?"

"Yes, if he's good and stops his digging!"

"He'll stop; won't you, Torry?"

The dog barked.

You could hear the dog yipping far down the street and away, going to fetch visitors. Martin was feverish and his eyes stood out in his head as he sat, propped up, listening, sending his mind rushing along with the dog, faster, faster. Yesterday Torry had brought Mrs. Holloway from Elm Avenue, with a story book for a present; the day before Torry had sat up, begged at Mr. Jacobs, the jeweler. Mr. Jacobs had bent and nearsightedly deciphered the tag message and, sure enough, had come shuffling and waddling to pay Martin a little how-do-you-do.

Now, Martin heard the dog returning through the smoky afternoon, barking, running, barking again.

Footsteps came lightly after the dog. Somebody

rang the downstairs bell, softly. Mom answered the door. Voices talked.

Torry raced upstairs, leaped on the bed. Martin leaned forward excitedly, his face shining, to see who'd come upstairs this time. Maybe Miss Palmborg or Mr. Ellis or Miss Jendriss, or—

The visitor walked upstairs, talking to Mom. It was a young woman's voice, talking with a laugh in it.

The door opened.

Martin had company.

Four days passed in which Torry did his job, reported morning, afternoon and evening temperatures, soil consistencies, leaf colors, rain levels, and, most important of all, brought visitors.

Miss Haight, again, on Saturday. She was the young, laughing, handsome woman with the gleaming brown hair and the soft way of walking. She lived in the big house on Park Street. It was her third visit in a month.

On Sunday it was Reverend Vollmar, on Monday Miss Clark and Mr. Henricks.

And to each of them Martin explained his dog. How in spring he was odorous of wild flowers and fresh earth; in summer he was baked, warm, sun-crisp; in autumn, now, a treasure trove of gold leaves hidden in his pelt for Martin to explore out. Torry demonstrated this process for the visitors, lying over on his back waiting to be explored.

Then, one morning, Mom told Martin about Miss Haight, the one who was so handsome and young and laughed.

She was dead.

Killed in a motoring accident in Glen Falls.

Martin held on to his dog, remembering Miss Haight, thinking of the way she smiled, thinking of her bright eyes, her closely cropped chestnut hair, her slim body, her quick walk, her nice stories about seasons and people.

So now she was dead. She wasn't going to laugh or tell stories any more. That's all there was to it. She was dead.

"What do they do in the graveyard, Mom, under the ground?"

"Nothing."

"You mean they just lay there?"

"Lie there," corrected Mom.

"*Lie* there . . . ?"

"Yes," said Mom, "that's all they do."

"It doesn't sound like much fun."

"It's not supposed to be."

"Why don't they get up and walk around once in a while if they get tired of lying there?"

"I think you've said enough, now," said Mom.

"I just wanted to know."

"Well, now you know."

"Sometimes I think God's pretty silly."

"Martin!"

Martin scowled. "You'd think He'd treat people better than throw dirt in their faces and tell them to lay still for keeps. You'd think He'd find a better way. What if I told Torry to play dead-dog? He does it awhile, but then he gets sick of it and wags his tail or blinks his eyes, or pants, or jumps off the bed, and walks around. I bet those graveyard people do the same, huh, Torry?"

Torry barked.

"That will do!" said Mom, firmly. "I don't like such talk!"

The autumn continued. Torry ran across forests, over the creek, prowling through the graveyard as

138

was his custom, and into town and around and back, missing nothing.

In mid-October, Torry began to act strangely. He couldn't seem to find anybody to come to visit Martin. Nobody seemed to pay attention to his begging. He came home seven days in a row without bringing a visitor. Martin was deeply despondent over it.

Mom explained it. "Everybody's busy. The war, and all. People have lots to worry over besides little begging dogs."

"Yeah," said Martin, "I guess so."

But there was more than that to it. Torry had a funny gleam in his eyes. As if he weren't really trying, or didn't care, or—something. Something Martin couldn't figure out. Maybe Torry was sick. Well, to heck with visitors. As long as he had Torry, everything was fine.

And then one day Torry ran out and didn't come back at all.

Martin waited quietly at first. Then—nervously. Then—anxiously.

At supper time he heard Mom and Dad call Torry. Nothing happened. It was no use. There was no sound of paws along the path outside the house. No sharp barking in the cold night air. Nothing. Torry was gone. Torry wasn't coming home—ever.

Leaves fell past the window. Martin sank on his pillow, slowly, a pain deep and hard in his chest.

The world was dead. There was no autumn because there was no fur to bring it into the house. There would be no winter because there would be no paws to dampen the quilt with snow. No more seasons. No more time. The go-between, the emissary, had been lost in the wild thronging of civilization, probably hit

139

by a car, or poisoned, or stolen, and there was no time.

Sobbing, Martin turned his face to his pillow. There was no contact with the world. The world was dead.

Martin twisted in bed and in three days the Halloween pumpkins were rotting in the trashcans, masks were burnt in incinerators, the bogeys were stacked away on shelves until next year. Halloween was withdrawn, impersonal, untouchable. It had simply been one evening when he had heard horns blowing off in the cold autumn stars, people yelling and thumping windows and porches with soap and cabbages. That was all.

Martin stared at the ceiling for the first three days of November, watching alternate light and dark shift across it. Days got shorter, darker, he could tell by the window. The trees were naked. The autumn wind changed its tempo and temperature. But it was just a pageant outside his window, nothing more. He couldn't get at it.

Martin read books about the seasons and the people in that world that was now nonexistent. He listened each day, but didn't hear the sounds he wanted to hear.

Friday night came. His parents were going to the theater. They'd be back at eleven. Miss Tarkins, from next door, would come over for a while until Martin got sleepy, and then she would go home.

Mom and Dad kissed him good night and walked out of the house into the autumn. He heard their footsteps go down the street.

Miss Tarkins came over, stayed awhile and then, when Martin confessed to being tired, she turned out all the lights and went back home.

Silence, then. Martin just lay there and watched

the stars moving slowly across the sky. It was a clear, moonlit evening. The kind when he and Torry had once run together across the town, across the sleeping graveyard, across the ravine, through the meadows, down the shadowed streets, chasing phantasmal childish dreams.

Only the wind was friendly. Stars don't bark. Trees don't sit up and beg. The wind, of course, did wag its tail against the house a number of times, startling Martin.

Now it was after nine o'clock.

If only Torry would come home, bringing some of the world with him. A burr or a rimed thistle, or the wind in his ears. If only Torry would come home.

And then, way off somewhere, there was a sound.

Martin arose in his covers, trembling. Starlight was reflected in his small eyes. He threw back the covers and tensed, listening.

There, again, was the sound.

It was so small it was like a needle point moving through the air miles and miles away.

It was the dreamy echo of a dog—barking.

It was the sound of a dog coming across meadows and fields, down dark streets, the sound of a dog running and letting his breath out to the night. The sound of a dog circling and running. It came and went, it lifted and faded, it came forward and went back, as if it were being led by someone on a chain. As if the dog were running and somebody whistled under the chestnut trees and the dog ran back, circled, and darted again for home.

Martin felt the room revolve under him and the bed tremble with his body. The springs complained with metal, tining voices.

The faint barking continued for five minutes, growing louder and louder.

141

Torry, come home! Torry, come home! Torry, boy, oh, Torry, where've you been? Oh, Torry, Torry!

Another five minutes. Nearer and nearer, and Martin kept saying the dog's name over and over again. Bad dog, wicked dog, to go off and leave him for all these days. Bad dog, good dog, come home, oh, Torry, hurry home and tell me about the world! Tears fell and dissolved into the quilt.

Nearer now. Very near. Just up the street, barking. Torry!

Martin held his breath. The sound of dog feet in the piled dry leaves, down the path. And now—right outside the house, barking, barking, barking! Torry!

Barking to the door.

Martin shivered. Did he dare run down and let the dog in, or should he wait for Mom and Dad to come home? Wait. Yes, he must wait. But it would be unbearable if, while he waited, the dog ran away again. No, he would go down and release the lock and his own special dog would leap into his arms again. Good Torry!

He started to move from bed when he heard the other sound. The door opened downstairs. Somebody was kind enough to have opened the door for Torry.

Torry had brought a visitor, of course. Mr. Buchanan, or Mr. Jacobs, or perhaps Miss Tarkins.

The door opened and closed and Torry came racing upstairs and flung himself, yipping, on the bed.

"Torry, where've you been, what've you done all this week?"

Martin laughed and cried all in one. He grabbed the dog and held him. Then he stopped laughing and crying, suddenly. He just stared at Torry with wide, strange eyes.

The odor arising from Torry was—different.

It was a smell of earth. Dead earth. Earth that had

142

lain cheek by jowl with unhealthy decaying things six feet under. Stinking, stinking, rancid earth. Clods of decaying soil fell off Torry's paws. And—something else—a small withered fragment of—*skin?*

Was it? Was it! WAS IT!

What kind of message was this from Torry? What did such a message mean? The stench—the ripe and awful cemetery earth.

Torry was a bad dog. Always digging where he shouldn't dig.

Torry was a *good* dog. Always making friends so easily. Torry took to liking everybody. He brought them home with him.

And now this latest visitor was coming up the stairs. Slowly. Dragging one foot after the other, painfully, slowly, slowly, slowly.

"Torry, Torry—where've you *been!*" screamed Martin.

A clod of rank crawling soil dropped from the dog's chest.

The door to the bedroom moved inward.

Martin had company.

▪William Sansom

Various Temptations

Out of the barren wastes of middle life a woman is tempted to play with passion, to trade the sterility of her routine existence for the lusty possibility of romantic love—all the more lusty, all the more tempting because of its possible danger.

HIS NAME UNKNOWN, he had been strangling girls in the Victoria district. After talking no one knew what to them by the gleam of brass bedsteads; after lonely hours standing on pavements with people passing; after perhaps in those hot July streets, with blue sky blinding high above and haze with burnt petrol, a dazzled head-aching hatred of some broad scarlet cinema poster and the black leather taxis; after sudden hopeless ecstasies at some rounded girl's figure passing in rubber and silk, after the hours of slow crumbs in the empty milk-bar and the balneal reek of grim-tiled lavatories? After all the day-town's

145

faceless hours, the evening town might have whirled quicker on him with the death of the day, the yellow-painted lights of the night have caused the minutes to accelerate and his fears to recede and a cold courage then to arm itself—until the wink, the terrible assent of some soft girl smiling toward the night . . . the beer, the port, the meat pies, the bedsteads?

Each of the four found had been throttled with coarse thread. This, dry and the color of hemp, had in each case been drawn from the frayed ends of the small carpet squares in those linoleum bedrooms. "A man," said the papers, "has been asked by the police to come forward in connection with the murders, etc., etc. . . . Ronald Raikes—five-foot-nine, gray eyes, thin brown hair, brown tweed coat, gray flannel trousers. Black soft-brim hat."

A girl called Clara, a plain girl and by profession an invisible mender, lay in her large white comfortable bed with its polished wood headpiece and its rose quilt. Faded blue curtains draped down their long soft cylinders, their dark recesses—and sometimes these columns moved, for the balcony windows were open for the hot July night. The night was still, airless; yet sometimes these queer causeless breezes, like the turning breath of a sleeper, came to rustle the curtains—and then as suddenly left them graven again in the stifling air like curtains that had never moved. And this girl Clara lay reading lazily the evening paper.

She wore an old wool bed jacket, faded yet rich against her pale and bloodless skin; she was alone, expecting no one. It was a night of restitution, of early supper and washing underclothes and stockings, an early night for a read and a long sleep.

Two or three magazines nestled in the eiderdowned bend of her knees. But saving for last the glossy, luxurious magazines, she lay now glancing through the paper—half reading, half tasting the quiet, sensing how secluded she was though the street was only one floor below, in her own bedroom yet with the heads of unsuspecting people passing only a few feet beneath. Unknown footsteps approached and retreated on the pavement beneath—footsteps that even on this still summer night sounded muffled, like footsteps heard on the pavement of a fog.

She lay listening for a while, then turned again to the paper, read again a bullying black headline relating the deaths of some hundreds of demonstrators somewhere in another hemisphere, and again let her eyes trail away from the weary grayish block of words beneath. The corner of the papers and its newsprint struck a harsh note of offices and tube-trains against the soft texture of the rose quilt—she frowned and was thus just about to reach for one of the more lustrous magazines when her eyes noted across the page a short, squat headline above a blackly typed column about the Victoria murders. She shuffled more comfortably into the bed and concentrated hard to scramble up the delicious paragraphs.

But they had found nothing. No new murder, nowhere nearer to making an arrest. Yet after an official preamble, there occurred one of those theoretic dissertations, such as is often inserted to color the progress of apprehension when no facts provide themselves. It appeared, it was thought, that the Victoria strangler suffered from a mania similar to that which had possessed the infamous Ripper; that is, the victims were mostly of a "certain profession"; it might be thus concluded that the

147

Victoria murderer bore the same maniacal grudge against such women.

At this Clara put the paper down—thinking, well, for one thing she never did herself up like those sort, in fact she never did herself up at all, and what would be the use? Instinctively then she turned to look across to the mirror on the dressing table, saw there her worn pale face and sack-colored hair, and felt instantly neglected; down in her plain-feeling body there stirred against that familiar envy, the impotent grudge that still came to her at least once every day of her life—that nobody had ever bothered to think deeply for her, neither loving, nor hating, nor in any way caring. For a moment then the thought came that whatever had happened in those bedrooms, however horrible, that murderer had at least felt deeply for his subject, the subject girl was charged with positive attractions that had forced him to act. There could hardly be such a thing, in those circumstances at least, as a disinterested murder. Hate and love were often held to be variations of the same obsessed emotion—when it came to murder, to the high impassioned pitch of murder, to such an intense concentration of one person on another, then it seemed that a divine paralysis, something very much like love, possessed the murderer.

Clara put the paper aside with finality, for whenever the question of her looks occurred, then she forced herself to think immediately of something else, to ignore what had for some years groaned into an obsession leading only to hours wasted with self-pity and idle depression. So that now she picked up the first magazine, and scrutinized with a false intensity the large and laughing figure in several colors and a few clothes of a motion-picture queen. However, rather than pointing her momentary depression, the picture comforted her. Had it been a real girl in the room, she might have been further saddened; but these pictures of fabulous people separated by the convention of the page and the distance of their world of celluloid fantasy instead represented the image of earlier personal dreams, comforting dreams of what then she hoped one day she might become, when that hope which is youth's unique asset outweighed the material attribute of what she in fact was.

In the quiet air fogging the room with such palpable stillness the turning of the brittle magazine page made its own decisive crackle. Somewhere outside in the summer night a car slurred past, changed its gear, rounded the corner and sped off on a petulant note of acceleration to nowhere. The girl changed her position in the bed, easing herself deeper into the security of the bedclothes. Gradually she became absorbed, so that soon her mind was again ready to wander, but this time within her own imagining, outside the plane of that bedroom. She was idly thus transported into a wished-for situation between herself and the owner of the shop where she worked: in fact, she spoke aloud her decision to take the following Saturday off. This her employer instantly refused. Then, still speaking aloud she presented her reasons, insisted—and at last, the blood beginning to throb in her forehead, handed in her notice! . . . This must have suddenly frightened her, bringing her back abruptly to the room—and she stopped talking. She laid the magazine down, looked around the room. Still that feeling of invisible fog— perhaps there was indeed mist; the furniture looked more than usually stationary. She tapped with her finger on the magazine. It sounded loud, too loud. Her mind returned to the murderer, she ceased tapping

149

and looked quickly at the shut door. The memory of those murders must have lain at the back of her mind throughout the past minutes, gently elevating her with the compounding unconscious excitement that news sometimes brings, the sensation that somewhere something has happened, revitalizing life. But now she suddenly shivered. Those murders had happened in Victoria, the neighboring district, only, in fact—she counted—five, six streets away.

The curtains began to move. Her eyes were round and at them in the first flickering moment. This time they not only shuddered, but seemed to eddy, and then to belly out. A coldness grasped and held the ventricles of her heart. And the curtains, the whole length of the rounded blue curtains moved toward her across the carpet. Something was pushing them. They traveled out toward her, then the ends rose sailing, sailed wide, opened to reveal nothing but the night, the empty balcony—then as suddenly collapsed and receded back to where they had hung motionless before. She let out the deep breath that, whitening, she had held all that time. Only, then, a breath of wind again; a curious swell on the compressed summer air. And now again the curtains hung still. She gulped sickly, crumpled and decided to shut the window—better not to risk that sort of fright again, one never knew what one's heart might do. But, just then, she hardly liked to approach those curtains. As the atmosphere of a nightmare cannot be shaken off for some minutes after waking, so those curtains held for a while their ambience of dread. Clara lay still. In a few minutes those fears quietened, but now forgetting the sense of fright, she made no attempt to leave the bed, it was too comfortable, she would read again for a little. She turned over and picked up her magazine. Then a short while later, stretching, she half-turned to the curtains again. They were wide open. A man was standing exactly in the center, outlined against the night outside, holding the curtains apart with his two hands.

Ron Raikes, five foot nine, gray eyes, thin brown hair, brown sports jacket, black hat, stood on the balcony holding the curtains aside looking in at this girl twisted around in her white-sheeted bed. He held the curtains slightly behind him, he knew the street to be dark, he felt safe. He wanted to breathe deeply after the short climb of the painter's ladder—but instead held it, above all kept quite still. The girl was staring straight at him, terrified, stuck in the pose of an actress suddenly revealed on her bedroom stage in its flood of light; in a moment she would scream. But something here was unusual, some quality lacking from the scene he had expected—and he concentrated, even in that moment when he knew himself to be in danger, letting some self-assured side of his mind wander and wonder what could be wrong.

He thought hard, screwing up his eyes to concentrate against the other unsteady excitements aching in his head—he knew how he had got here, he remembered the dull disconsolate hours waiting around the station, following two girls without result, then walking away from the lighted crowds into these darker streets and suddenly seeing a glimpse of this girl through the lighted window. Then that curious, unreasoned idea had crept over him. He had seen the ladder, measured the distance, then scoffed at himself for risking such an escapade. Anyone might have seen him . . . and then what, arrest for house-breaking, burglary? He had turned, walked away. Then walked back. That extraordinary excite-

151

ment rose and held him. He had gritted his teeth, told himself not to be such a fool, to go home. Tomorrow would be fresh, a fine day to spend. But then the next hours of the restless night exhibited themselves, sounding their emptiness—so that it had seemed too early to give in and admit the day worthless. A sensation then of ability, of dextrous clever power had taken him—he had loitered nearer the ladder, looking up and down the street. The lamps were dull, the street empty. Once a car came slurring past, changed gear, accelerated off petulantly into the night, away to nowhere. The sound emphasized the quiet, the protection of that deserted hour. He had put a hand on the ladder. It was then the same as any simple choice—taking a drink or not taking a drink. The one action might lead to some detrimental end— to more drinks, a night out, a headache in the morning—and would thus be best avoided; but the other, that action of taking, was pleasant and easy, and the moral forehead argued that after all it could do no harm. So, quickly, telling himself he would climb down again in a second, this man Raikes had prised himself above the lashed night-plank and had run up the ladder. On the balcony he had paused by the curtains, breathless, now exhilarated in his ability, agile and alert as an animal—and had heard the sound of the girl turning in bed and the flick of her magazine page. A moment later the curtains had moved, nimbly he had stepped aside. A wind. He had looked down at the street—the wind populated the curbs with dangerous movement. He parted the curtains, saw the girl lying there alone, and silently stepped onto the threshold.

Now when at last she screamed—a hoarse diminutive sob—he knew he must move, and so soundlessly on the carpet went toward her. As he

152

moved he spoke: "I don't want to hurt you"—and then, knowing that he must say something more than that, which she could hardly have believed, and knowing also that above all he must keep talking all the time with no pause to let her attention scream— "Really I don't want to hurt you, you mustn't scream, let me explain—but don't you see if you scream I shall have to stop you. . . ." Even with a smile, as soft a gesture as his soft-speaking voice, he pushed forward his coat pocket, his hand inside, so that the girl might recognize what she must have seen in detective stories, and even believe it to be his hand and perhaps a pipe, yet not be sure: ". . . but I won't shoot and you'll promise, won't you, to be good and not scream—while I tell you why I'm here. You think I'm a burglar, that's not true. It's right I need a little money, only a little cash, ten bob even, because I'm in trouble, not dangerous trouble, but let me tell you, please, please listen to me, miss." His voice continued softly talking, talking all the time quietly and never stuttering nor hesitating nor leaving a pause. Gradually, though her body remained alert and rigid, the girl's face relaxed.

He stood at the foot of the bed, in the full light of the bedside lamp, leaning awkwardly on one leg, the cheap material of his coat ruffled and papery. Still talking, always talking, he took off his hat, lowered himself gently to sit on the end of the bed—rather to put her at her ease than to encroach further for himself. As he sat, he apologized. Then, never pausing, he told her a story, which was nearly true, about his escape from a detention camp, the cruelty of his long sentence for a trivial theft, the days thereafter of evasion, the furtive search for casual employment, and then, worst of all, the long hours of time on his hands, the vacuum of time wandering,

153

time wasting on the café clocks, lamp posts of time waiting on blind corners, time walking away from uniforms, time of the head-aching clocks loitering at the slow pace of death toward his sole refuge—sleep. And this was nearly true—only that he omitted that his original crime had been one of sexual assault; he omitted these events because in fact he had forgotten them, they could only be recollected with difficulty, as episodes of vague elation, dark and blurred as an undeveloped photograph of which the image should be known yet puzzles with its indeterminate shape, its hints of light in the darkness and always the feeling that it should be known, that it once surely existed. This was also like anyone trying to remember exactly what had been done between any two specific hours on some date of a previous month, two hours framed by known engagements yet themselves blurred into an exasperating and hungry screen of dots, dark, almost appearing, convolving, receding.

So gradually as he offered himself to the girl's pity, that bedclothes hump of figure relaxed. Once her lips flexed their corners in the beginning of a smile. Into her eyes once crept that strange coquettish look, pained and immeasurably tender, with which a woman takes into her arms a strange child. The moment of danger was past, there would be no scream. And since now on her part she seemed to feel no danger from him, then it became very possible that the predicament might even appeal to her, to any girl nourished by the kind of drama that filled the magazines littering her bed. As well, he might look strained and ill—so he let his shoulders droop for the soft extraction of her last sympathy.

Yet as he talked on, as twice he instilled into the endless story a compliment to her and as twice her

154

face seemed to shine for a moment with sudden life—nevertheless he sensed that all was not right with this apparently well-contrived affair. For this, he knew, should be near the time when he would be edging nearer to her, dropping his hat, picking it up and shifting thus unostensibly his position. It was near the time when he would be near enough to attempt, in one movement, the risk that could never fail, either way, accepted or rejected. But . . . he was neither moving forward nor wishing to move. Still he talked, but now more slowly, with less purpose; he found that he was looking at her detachedly, no longer mixing her image with his words—and thus losing the words their energy; looking now not at the conceived image of something painted by the desiring brain—but as at something unexpected, not entirely known; as if instead of peering forward, his head were leaned back, surveying, listening, as a dog perhaps leans its head to one side listening for the whistled sign to regulate the bewildering moment. But—no such sign came. And through his words, straining at the diamond cunning that maintained him, he tried to reason out this perplexity, he annotated carefully what he saw. A white face, ill-white, reddened faintly around the nostrils, pink and dry at the mouth; and a small fat mouth, puckered and fixed under its long upper lip; and eyes also small, yet full-irised and thus like brown pellets under eyebrows low and thick: and hair that color of lusterless hemp, now tied with a bow so that it fell down either side of her cheeks as lank string: and around her thin neck, a thin gold chain just glittering above the dull blue wool of that bedjacket, blue brittle wool against the ill white skin: and behind, a white pillow and the dark wooden head of the bed curved like an inverted shield. Unattractive . . . not

155

attractive as expected, not exciting . . . yet where? Where before had he remembered something like this, something impelling, strangely sympathetic and— there was no doubt—earnestly wanted?

Later, in contrast, there flashed across his memory the color of other faces—a momentary reflection from the scarlet-lipped face on one of the magazine covers—and he remembered that these indeed troubled him, but in a different and accustomed way; these pricked at him in their busy way, lanced him hot, ached into his head so that it grew light, as in strong sunlight. And then, much later, long after this girl too had nervously begun to talk, after they had talked together, they made a cup of tea in her kitchen. And then, since the July dawn showed through the curtains, she made a bed for him on the sofa in the sitting room, a bed of blankets and a silk cushion for his head.

Two weeks later the girl Clara came home at five o'clock in the afternoon carrying three parcels. They contained two colored ties, six yards of white material for her wedding dress, and a box of thin red candles.

As she walked toward her front door she looked up at the windows and saw that they were shut. As it should have been—Ron was out as he had promised. It was his birthday. Thirty-two. For a few hours Clara was to concentrate on giving him a birthday tea, forgetting for one evening the fabulous question of that wedding dress. Now she ran up the stairs, opened the second door and saw there in an instant that the flat had been left especially clean, tidied into a straight, unfamiliar rigor. She smiled (how thoughtful he was, despite his "strangeness") and threw her parcels down on the sofa, disarranging the cushions, in her tolerant happiness delighting in this. Then she was up again and arranging things. First the lights—silk handkerchiefs wound over the tops of the shades, for they shone too brightly. Next the tablecloth, white and fresh, soon decorated with small tinsels left over from Christmas, red crackers with feathered paper ends, globes gleaming like crimson quicksilver, silver and copper snowflakes.

(He'll like this, a dash of color. It's his birthday, perhaps we could have gone out, but in a way it's nicer in. Anyway, it must be in with him on the run. I wonder where he is now. I hope he went straight to the pictures. In the dark it's safe. We did have fun doing him up different—a nice blue suit, distinguished—and the mustache is nice. Funny how you get used to that, he looks just the same as that first night. Quite a quiet one. Says he likes to be quiet too, a plain life and a peaceful one. But a spot of color—oh, it'll do him good.)

Moving efficiently, she hurried to the kitchen and fetched the hidden cake, placed it exactly in the center of the table, wound a length of gold veiling around the bottom, undid the candle parcel, and expertly set the candles—one to thirty-one—around the white-iced circle. She wanted to light them, but instead put down the matches and picked off the cake one silver pellet and placed this on the tip of her tongue: then impatiently went for the knives and forks. All these actions were performed with that economy and swiftness of movement peculiar to women who arrange their own houses, a movement so sure that it seems to suggest dislike. So that it brings with each adjustment a grimace of disapproval, though nothing by anyone could be more approved.

(Thirty-one candles—I won't put the other one, it's nicer for him to think he's still thirty-one. Or I suppose men don't mind—still, do it. You never know what he really likes. A quiet one—but ever so thoughtful. And tender. And that's a funny thing, you'd think he might have tried something, the way he is, on the loose. A regular Mr. Proper. Doesn't like this, doesn't like that, doesn't like dancing, doesn't like the way the girls go about, doesn't like lipstick, nor the way some of them dress . . . of course he's right, they make themselves up plain silly, but you'd think a man . . .?)

Now over to the sideboard, and from that polished oak cupboard take very carefully one, two, three, four fat quart bottles of black stout—and a half bottle of port. Group them close together on the table, put the shining glasses just by, make it look like a real party. And the cigarettes, a colored box of fifty. Crinkly paper serviettes. And last of all a long roll of paper, vivid green, on which she had traced, with a ruler and a pot of red paint: HAPPY BIRTHDAY, RON!

This was now hung between two wall lights, old gas jets corded with electricity and shaded—and then she went to the door and switched on all the lights. The room warmed instantly, each light threw off a dark glow, as though it were part of its own shadow. Clara went to the curtains and half drew them, cutting off some of the daylight. Then drew them altogether—and the table gleamed into sudden night-light, golden white and warmly red, with the silver cake sparkling in the center. She went into the other room to dress.

Sitting by the table with the mirror she took off her hat and shook her head; in the mirror the hair seemed to tumble about, not pinned severely as usual, but free and flopping—she had had it waved. The face, freckled with pinpoints of the mirror's tarnish, looked pale and far away. She remembered she had much to do, and turned busily to a new silk blouse, hoping that Ron would still be in the pictures, beginning again to think of him.

She was not certain still that he might not be the man whom the police wanted in connection with those murders. She had thought it, of course, when he first appeared. Later his tender manner had dissipated such a first impression. He had come to supper the following night, and again stayed; thus also for the next nights. It was understood that she was giving him sanctuary—and for his part, he insisted on paying her when he could again risk inquiring for work. It was an exciting predicament, of the utmost daring for anyone of Clara's way of life. Incredible—but the one important and over-riding fact had been that suddenly, even in this shocking way, there had appeared a strangely attractive man who had expressed immediately an interest in her. She knew that he was also interested in his safety. But there was much more to his manner than simply this—his tenderness and his extraordinary preoccupation with her, staring, listening, striving to please and addressing to her all the attentions of which through her declining youth she had been starved. She knew, moreover, that these attentions were real and not affected. Had they been false, nevertheless she would have been flattered. But as it was, the new horizons became dreamlike, drunken, impossible. To a normally frustrated, normally satisfied, normally hopeful woman—the immoral possibility that he might be that murderer would have frozen the relationship in its seed. But such was the waste and the want in lonely Clara that, despite every ingrained convention, the great boredom of her dull years had seemed to gather and move inside her, had heaved itself up like a monstrous sleeper turning,

159

rearing and then subsiding on its other side with a flop of finality, a sigh of pleasure, welcoming now anything, anything but a return to the old dull days of nothing. There came the whisper: "Now or never!" But there was no sense, as with other middle-aged escapists, of desperation; this chance had landed squarely on her doorstep, there was no striving, no doubt—it had simply happened. Then the instinctive knowledge of love—and finally, to seal the atrophy of all hesitation, his proposal of marriage. So that now when she sometimes wondered whether he was the man the police wanted, her loyalty to him was so deeply assumed that it seemed she was really thinking of somebody else—or of him as another figure at a remove of time. The murders had certainly stopped—yet only two weeks ago? And anyway the man in the tweed coat was only wanted *in connection with* the murders . . . that in itself became indefinite . . . besides, there must be thousands of tweed coats and black hats . . . and besides there were thousands of coincidences of all kinds every day. . . .

So, shrugging her shoulders and smiling at herself for puzzling her mind so—when she knew there could be no answer—she returned to her dressing table. Here her face grew serious, as again the lips pouted and down-drawn disapproval that meant she contemplated an act of which she approved. Her hand hesitated, then opened one of the dressing-table drawers. It disappeared inside, feeling to the very end of the drawer, searching there in the dark. Her lips parted, her eyes lost focus—as though she were scratching deliciously her back. At length the hand drew forth a small parcel.

Once more she hesitated, while the fingers itched at the knotted string. Suddenly they took hold of the knot and scrambled to untie it. The brown paper

160

parted. Inside lay a lipstick and a box of powder. (Just a little, a very little. I must look pretty. I *must* tonight.)

She pouted her lips and drew across them a thick scarlet smear, then frowned, exasperated by such extravagance. She started to wipe it off. But it left, boldly impregnated already, its mark. She shrugged her shoulders, looked fixedly into the mirror. What she saw pleased her, and she smiled.

As late as seven, when it was still light but the strength had left the day, when on trees and on the gardens of squares there extended a moist and cool shadow and even over the tram-torn streets a cooling sense of business past descended—Ronald Raikes left the cinema and hurried to get through the traffic and away into those quieter streets that led toward Clara's flat. After a day of gritted heat, the sky was clouding; a few shops and orange-painted snack bars had turned on their electric lights. By these lights and the homing hurry of the traffic, Raikes felt the presence of the evening, and clenched his jaw against it. That restlessness, vague as the hot breath before a headache, lightly metallic as the taste of fever, must be avoided. He skirted the traffic dangerously, hurrying for the quieter streets away from that garish junction. Between the green and purple tiles of a public house and the red-framed window of a passport photographer's he entered at last into the duller, quieter perspective of a street of brown brick houses. Here was instant relief, as though a draft of wind had cooled physically his head. He thought of the girl, the calm flat, the safety, the rightness and the sanctuary there. Extraordinary, this sense of rightness and order that he felt with her: ease, relief, and constant need. Not at all like "being in love."

161

Like being very young again, with a protective nurse. Looking down at the pavement cracks he felt pleasure in them, pleasure reflected from a sense of gratitude—and he started planning, to get a job next week, to end this hiding about, to do something for her in return. And then he remembered that even at that moment she was doing something more for him, arranging some sort of treat, a birthday supper. And thus tenderly grateful, he slipped open the front door and climbed the stairs.

There were two rooms—the sitting room and the bedroom. He tried the sitting-room door, which was regarded as his, but found it locked. But in the instant of rattling the knob Clara's voice came: "Ron? . . . Ron, go in the bedroom, put your hat there—don't come in till you're quite ready. Surprise!"

Out in the dark passage, looking down at the brownish bare linoleum, he smiled again, nodded, called a greeting and went into the bedroom. He washed, combed his hair, glancing now and then toward the closed connecting door. At last look in the mirror, a nervous washing gesture of his hands, and he was over at the door and opening it.

Coming from the daylit bedroom, this other room appeared like a picture of night, like some dimly-lit tableau recessed in a waxwork-show. He was momentarily dazzled not by light but by a yellow darkness, a promise of other unfocused light, the murky bewilderment of a room entered from strong sunlight. But a voice sang out to help him: "Ron—Happy Birthday!" and, reassured, his eyes began to assemble the room—the table, crackers, shining cake, glasses and bottles, the green paper greeting, the glittering tinsel and those downcast shaded lights. Around the cake burned the little upright knives of those thirty-one candles, each yellow blade winking. The ceiling disappeared in darkness, all the light was lowered down upon the table and the carpet. He stood for a moment still shocked, robbed still of the room he had expected, its cold and clockless daylight, its motionless smell of dust.

An uncertain figure that was Clara came forward from behind the table, her waist and legs in light, then upward in shadow. Her hand stretched toward him, her voice laughed from the darkness. And thus with the affirmation of her presence, the feeling of shock mysteriously cleared, the room fell into a different perspective—and instantly he saw with gratitude how carefully she had arranged that festive table, indeed how prettily reminiscent it was of festivity, old Christmases and parties held long ago in some separate life. Happier, he was able to watch the glasses fill with rich black stout, saw the red wink of the port dropped in to sweeten it, raised his glass in a toast. Then they stood in the half-light of that upper shadow, drank, joked, talked themselves into the climate of celebration. They moved around that table with its bright low center light like figures about a shaded gambling board—so vivid the clarity of their lowered hands, the sheen of his suit and the gleam of her stockings, yet with their faces veiled and diffused. Then, when two of the bottles were already empty, they sat down.

Raikes blinked in the new light. Everything sparkled suddenly, all things around him seemed to wink. He laughed, abruptly too excited. Clara was bending away from him, stretching to cut the cake. As he raised his glass, he saw from the corner of his eye, over the crystal rim of his glass—and held it then undrunk. He stared at the shining white blouse, the concisely corrugated folds of the knife-edge wave of her hair. Clara? The strangeness of the room

163

dropped its curtain around him again, heavily. Clara, a slow voice mentioned in his mind, has merely bought herself a new blouse and waved her hair. He nodded, accepting this automatically. But the stout to which he was not used to weighed inside his head, as though some heavy circular hat were being pressed down, wreathing leadenly where its brim circled, forcing a lightness within that seemed to balloon airily upward. Unconsciously his hand went to his forehead—and at that moment Clara turned her face toward him, setting it on one side in the full light, blowing out some of those little red candles, laughing as she blew. The candle flames flickered and winked like jewels close to her cheek. She blew her cheeks out, so that they became full and rounded, then laughed so that her white teeth gleamed between oil-rich red lips.

Thin candle-threads of black smoke needled curling by her hair. She saw something strange in his eyes. Her voice said: "Why, Ron—you haven't a headache? Not yet anyway . . . eh, dear?"

Now he no longer laughed naturally, but felt the stretch of his lips as he tried to smile a denial of the headache. The worry was at his head, he felt no longer at ease in that familiar chair, but rather balanced on it alertly, so that under the table his calves were braced, so that he moved his hands carefully for fear of encroaching on what was not his, hands of a guest, hands uneasy at a strange table.

Clara sat around now facing him—their chairs were to the same side of that round table, and close. She kept smiling; those new things she wore were plainly stimulating her, she must have felt transformed and beautiful. Such a certainty, together with the unaccustomed alcohol, brought a vivacity to her eye, a definition to the movements of her mouth.

164

Traces of faltering, of apology, of all the wounded humilities of a face that apologizes for itself—all these were gone, wiped away beneath the white powder; now her face seemed to be charged with light, expressive, and in its new self-assurance predatory. It was a face bent on effect, on making its mischief. Instinctively it performed new tricks, attitudes learned and stored but never before used, the intuitive mimicry of the female seducer. She smiled now largely, as though her lips enjoyed the touch of her teeth; lowered her eyelids, then sprang them suddenly open; ended a laugh by tossing her head—only to shake the new curls in the light; raised her hand to her throat, to show the throat stretched back and soft, took a piece of butter-colored marzipan and its marble-white icing between the tips of two fingers and, laughing, opened her mouth very wide and then suddenly shut in a coy gobble. And all this time, while they ate and drank and talked and joked, Raikes sat watching her, smiling his lips, but eyes heavily bright and fixed like pewter as the trouble roasted his brain.

He knew now fully what he wanted to do. His hand, as if it were some other hand not connected to his body, reached away to where the parcel of ties lay open; and its fingers were playing with the string. They played with it overwillingly, like fingers guiding a paintbrush to overdecorate a picture, like fingers that pour more salt into a well-seasoned cookpot. Against the knowledge of what he wanted, the mind still balanced its danger, calculated the result and its difficult aftermath. Once again this was gluttonous, like deciding to take more drink. Sense of the moment, imagination of the result; the moment's desire, the mind's warning. Twice he leaned toward her, measuring the distance, then

165

drawing back. His mind told him that he was playing, he was allowed such play, nothing would come of it.

Then abruptly it happened. That playing, like a swing pushing higher and then somersaulting the circle, mounted on its own momentum, grew huge and boundless, swelled like fired gas. Those fingers tautened, snapped the string. He was up off the chair and over Clara. The string, sharp and hempen, bit into her neck. Her lips opened in a wide laugh, for she thought he was clowning up suddenly to kiss her, and then stretched themselves wider, then closed into a bluish cough and the last little sounds.

166

▪Ella Wilkinson Peattie

The Grammatical Ghost

Exorcism of a ghost can be accomplished by many means. Call in a medium to liberate the tormented spirit. Use fire and incantations. Employ sheer force of will, setting one spirit against another. But the ghost that appears here is exorcised in a manner all its own.

THERE WAS ONLY ONE possible objection to the drawing room, and that was the occasional presence of Miss Carew; and only one possible objection to Miss Carew. And that was, that she was dead.

She had been dead twenty years, as a matter of fact and record, and to the last of her life sacredly preserved the treasures and traditions of her family, a family bound up—as it is quite unnecessary to explain to anyone in good society—with all that is most venerable and heroic in the history of the Republic. Miss Carew never relaxed the proverbial

167

hospitality of her house, even when she remained its sole representative. She continued to preside at her table with dignity and state, and to set an example of excessive modesty and gentle decorum to a generation of restless young women.

It is not likely that, having lived a life of such irreproachable gentility as this, Miss Carew would have the bad taste to die in any way not pleasant to mention in fastidious society. She could be trusted to the last, not to outrage those friends who quoted her as an exemplar of propriety. She died very unobtrusively of an affection of the heart, one June morning, while trimming her rose trellis, and her lavender-colored print was not even rumpled when she fell, nor were more than the tips of her little bronze slippers visible.

"Isn't it dreadful," said the Philadelphians, "that the property should go to a very, very distant cousin in Iowa or somewhere else on the frontier, about whom nobody knows anything at all?"

The Carew treasures were packed in boxes and sent away into the Iowa wilderness; the Carew traditions were preserved by the Historical Society; the Carew property, standing in one of the most umbrageous and aristocratic suburbs of Philadelphia, was rented to all manner of folk—anybody who had money enough to pay the rental—and society entered its doors no more.

But at last, after twenty years, and when all save the oldest Philadelphians had forgotten Miss Lydia Carew, the very, very distant cousin appeared. He was quite in the prime of life, and agreeable and unassuming. With him were two maiden sisters, ladies of excellent taste and manners, who restored the Carew china to its ancient cabinets and replaced the Carew pictures upon the walls, with additions not

168

out of keeping with the elegance of these heirlooms. Society, with a magnanimity almost dramatic, overlooked his name of Boggs—and called.

All was well. At least, to an outsider all seemed to be well. But, in truth, there was a certain distress in the old mansion, and in the hearts of the well-behaved Misses Boggs. It came about most unexpectedly.

The sisters had been sitting upstairs, looking out at the beautiful grounds of the old place, and marveling at the violets which lifted their heads from every possible cranny about the house, and talking over the cordiality which they had been receiving by those upon whom they had no claim, and they were filled with amiable satisfaction. Life looked attractive. They had often been grateful to Miss Lydia Carew for leaving their brother her fortune. Now they felt even more grateful to her. She had left them a Social Position—one, which even after twenty years of disuse, was fit for use.

They descended the stairs together, with arms clasped about each other's waists, and as they did so presented a placid and pleasing sight. They entered their drawing room with the intention of brewing a cup of tea, and drinking it in calm sociability in the twilight. But as they entered the room they became aware of the presence of a lady, who was already seated at their tea table, regarding their old Wedgwood with the air of a connoisseur.

There were a number of peculiarities about this intruder. To begin with, she was hatless, quite as if she were a habitué of the house, and was costumed in a prim lilac-colored lawn of the style of two decades past. But a greater peculiarity was the resemblance this lady bore to a faded daguerrotype. If looked at one way, she was perfectly discernible; if looked at

169

another, she went out in a sort of blur. Notwithstanding this comparative invisibility, she exhaled a delicate perfume of sweet lavender, very pleasing to the nostrils of the Misses Boggs, who stood looking at her in gentle and unprotesting surprise.

"I beg your pardon," began Miss Prudence, the younger of the Misses Boggs, "but—"

But at this moment the daguerrotype became a blur, and Miss Prudence found herself addressing space. The Misses Boggs were irritated. They had never encountered any mysteries in Iowa. They began an impatient search behind doors and portieres, and even under sofas, though it was quite absurd to suppose that a lady recognizing the merits of the Carew Wedgwood would so far forget herself as to crawl under a sofa.

When they had given up all hope of discovering the intruder, they saw her standing at the far end of the drawing room critically examining a watercolor marine. The elder Miss Boggs started toward her with stern decision, but the little daguerrotype turned with a shadowy smile, became a blur and an imperceptibility.

Miss Boggs looked at Miss Prudence Boggs.

"If there *were* ghosts," she said, "this would be one."

"If there *were* ghosts," said Miss Prudence Boggs, "this would be the ghost of Lydia Carew."

The twilight was settling into the blackness, and Miss Boggs nervously lit the gas while Miss Prudence ran for other teacups, preferring, for reasons superfluous to mention, not to drink out of the Carew china that evening.

The next day, on taking up her embroidery frame, Miss Boggs found a number of old-fashioned cross-

170

stitches added to her own stitches. Prudence, she knew, would never have degraded herself by taking a cross-stitch, and the parlormaid was above taking such a liberty. Miss Boggs mentioned the incident that night at a dinner given by an ancient friend of the Carews.

"Oh, that's the work of Lydia Carew, without a doubt!" cried the hostess. "She visits every new family that moves to the house, but she never remains more than a week or two with anyone."

"It must be that she disapproves of them," suggested Miss Boggs.

"I think that's it," said the hostess. "She doesn't like their china, or their fiction."

"I hope she'll disapprove of us," added Miss Prudence.

The hostess belonged to a very old Philadelphian family, and she shook her head.

"I should say it was a compliment for even the ghost of Miss Lydia Carew to approve of one," she said severely.

The next morning, when the sisters entered their drawing room there were numerous evidences of an occupant during their absence. The sofa pillows had been rearranged so that the effect of their grouping was less bizarre than that favored by the Western women; a horrid little Buddhist idol, with its eyes fixed on its abdomen, had been chastely hidden behind a Dresden shepherdess, as unfit for the scrutiny of polite eyes; and on the table where Miss Prudence did work in watercolors, after the fashion of the Impressionists, lay a prim and impossible composition representing a moss rose and a number of heartsease, colored with that caution which modest spinster artists instinctively exercise.

"Oh, there's no doubt it's the work of Miss Lydia Carew," said Miss Prudence, contemptuously. "There's no mistaking the drawing of that rigid little rose. Don't you remember those wreaths and bouquets framed, among the pictures we got when the Carew pictures were sent to us? I gave some of them to an orphan asylum and burned the rest."

"Hush!" cried Miss Boggs, involuntarily. "If she heard you, it would hurt her feelings terribly. Of course, I mean—" and she blushed. "It *might* hurt her feelings—but how perfectly ridiculous! It's impossible!"

Miss Prudence held up the sketch of the moss rose.

"That may be impossible in an artistic sense, but it *is* a palpable thing."

"Bosh!" cried Miss Boggs.

"But," protested Miss Prudence, "how do you explain it?"

"I don't," said Miss Boggs, and left the room.

That evening the sisters made a point of being in the drawing room before the dusk came on, and of lighting the gas at the first hint of twilight. They didn't believe in Miss Lydia Carew—but still they meant to be beforehand with her. They talked with unwonted vivacity and in a louder tone than was their custom. But as they drank their tea, even their utmost verbosity could not make them oblivious to the fact that the perfume of sweet lavender was stealing insidiously through the room. They tacitly refused to recognize this odor and all that it indicated, when suddenly, with a sharp crash, one of the old Carew teacups fell from the tea table to the floor and was broken. The disaster was followed by what sounded like a sign of pain and dismay.

"I didn't suppose Miss Lydia would ever be as

172

awkward as that," cried the younger Miss Boggs, petulantly.

"Prudence," said her sister with a stern accent, "please try not to be a fool. You brushed the cup off with the sleeve of your dress."

"Your theory wouldn't be so bad," said Miss Prudence, half laughing and half crying, "if there were any sleeves to my dress, but, as you see, there aren't," and then Miss Prudence had something as near hysterics as a healthy young woman from the West can have.

"I wouldn't think such a perfect lady as Lydia Carew," she ejaculated between her sobs, "would make herself so disagreeable! You may talk about good breeding all you please, but I call such intrusion exceedingly bad taste. I have a horrible idea that she likes us and means to stay with us. She left those other people because she did not approve of their habits or their grammar. It would be just our luck to please her."

"Well, I like your egotism," said Miss Boggs.

However, the view Miss Prudence took of the case appeared to be the right one. Time went by and Miss Lydia Carew still remained. When the ladies entered their drawing room they would see the little ladylike daguerrotype revolving itself into a blur before one of the family portraits. Or they noticed that the yellow sofa cushion, toward which she appeared to feel a peculiar antipathy, had been dropped behind the sofa upon the floor; or that one of Jane Austen's novels, which none of the family ever read, had been removed from the book shelves and left open upon the table.

"I cannot become reconciled to it," complained Miss Boggs to Miss Prudence. "I wish we had remained in Iowa where we belong. Of course I don't believe in the thing! No sensible person would. But still I cannot become reconciled."

But their liberation was to come, and in a most unexpected manner.

A relative by marriage visited them from the West. He was a friendly man and had much to say, so he talked all through dinner, and afterward followed the ladies to the drawing room to finish his gossip. The gas in the room was turned very low, and as they entered, Miss Prudence caught sight of Miss Carew, in company attire, sitting in upright propriety in a stiff-backed chair at the extremity of the room.

Miss Prudence had a sudden idea.

"We will not turn up the gas," she said, with an emphasis intended to convey private information to her sister. "It will be more agreeable to sit here and talk in this soft light."

Neither her brother nor the man from the West made any objection. Miss Boggs and Miss Prudence, clasping each other's hands, divided their attention between their corporeal and their incorporeal guests. Miss Boggs was confident that her sister had an idea, and was willing to await its development. As the guest from Iowa spoke, Miss Carew bent a politely attentive ear to what he said.

"Ever since Richards took sick that time," he said briskly, "it seemed like he shed all responsibility." (The Misses Boggs saw the daguerrotype put up her shadowy head with a movement of doubt and apprehension.)

"The fact of the matter was, Richards didn't seem to scarcely get on the way he might have been expected to." (At this conscienceless split of the

174

infinitive and misplacing of the preposition, Miss Carew arose, trembling perceptibly.)

"I saw it wasn't no use for him to count on a quick recovery—"

The Misses Boggs lost the rest of the sentence, for at the utterance of the double negative Miss Lydia Carew had flashed out, not in a blur, but with mortal haste, as when life goes out at a pistol shot!

The man from the West wondered why Miss Prudence should have cried at so pathetic a part of his story:

"Thank goodness!"

And their brother was amazed to see Miss Boggs kiss Miss Prudence with passion and energy.

It was the end. Miss Carew returned no more.

▪August Derleth

The Patchwork Quilt

A child's patchwork quilt—which seems to have a life of its own—floats up from the foot of the bed to keep the occupant warm. But who is the mysterious figure that tucks her in?

IN THE SECOND NIGHT of Ariel Bennett's visit to her aunts, the weather turned cold. She woke from sleep, feeling it in this old house to which her aunts had come to live during the year just past, and lay for a few minutes trying to imagine herself warming, trying to believe that the chill would pass. But the room was cold; there was no denying it; so she got resolutely out of bed and turned on the lamp so that she could look about for something to add to the thin covers on the bed. She regretted now that she had left her coat hanging downstairs, and she would not disturb either Aunt Ellen or Aunt Beatrice by leaving her room to go for it.

176

She opened one drawer after another of the old-fashioned high bureau against the wall. There were sheets and pillowcases, but no blankets. She looked into the closet. It was empty save for a cardboard carton pushed away in one corner of the overhead shelf. She was about to turn away when, on impulse, she turned and took down the carton.

She carried it into the room, untied the string around it, and opened it. A kind of tissue paper met her eyes, yellowing and old. She pushed it aside and was immediately gratified at the sight of what could be only a quilt, handmade of patchwork. As she took it out of the carton, she could see that it was almost new, virtually unused, and of exquisite workmanship, in a pattern of blues and reds and dark gray.

Without hesitation, she spread it over the bed, put out the light, and got back into bed once more, snuggling into the warmed spot she had left.

Within a few minutes she was alseep once more.

She woke again in an hour, uncomfortably warm. Somehow the quilt had bunched up over her shoulders and drawn up from her feet, so that her feet, at the same time that her head and shoulders were overly warm, were chill. She straightened the blanket carefully, without getting out of bed to do it, and settled back.

By this time she had worn off the edge of the need to sleep, and getting back to sleep took longer. The moonlight from outside made a pale luminosity in the room, making a parallelogram on the floor immediately off the sill of the one window in the south wall, and along the eastern horizon there was just the hint that dawn was not far away. Far off somewhere across the fields a dog barked, and a errant rooster crowed; all else was silence.

She waited upon sleep to come again, growing

177

slowly drowsy. The room dimmed and darkened, her eyelids lowered. On the outer boundary of sleep she thought she saw one of her aunts bending over the bed, tucking the blanket in; she smiled but was too close to sleep to speak.

In the morning she folded the patchwork quilt and lay it across the bottom of the bed. Then she went downstairs, refreshed.

Her aunts were up. Aunt Beatrice was just pouring coffee; Aunt Ellen was in the pantry.

"Good morning, dear," said Aunt Beatrice, her thin face lit with a smile. "Did you sleep well?"

"Oh, yes, of course," she answered. "I was a little cold at first, but after I put the quilt on, I was warm enough."

"That's good," said Aunt Beatrice. "There's some real cream for your coffee, Ariel." She pushed the pitcher toward her.

Aunt Ellen bustled in from the pantry and plumped her fat little body into her chair. "It *was* cold last night. The weather does turn fast sometimes like this in Vermont."

"All over New England," said Aunt Beatrice.

"We should have thought to leave an extra blanket on your bed," Aunt Ellen went on.

Aunt Beatrice paused in the act of stirring the sugar in her coffee. She looked blankly at her niece. "What quilt?" she asked suddenly.

"The one in the closet," said Ariel.

Aunt Beatrice took the spoon from her cup and laid it carefully beside her plate. She looked across the table at her sister. For a moment neither of them spoke a word. A sort of restraint seemed to have fallen upon the breakfast table.

"It was just a patchwork quilt," Ariel went on. "I

didn't think you'd mind if I used it. Of course, I realized it was put away, but it was a perfectly good quilt—almost like new. I thought," she ended lamely, "you knew I had it on the bed. Didn't one of you come in during the night to tuck it in?"

Aunt Beatrice ignored her question. "That quilt was in the house when we came here. It's not really ours. I don't think we ought to use it. We always understood someone would come for it."

"Yes," put in Aunt Ellen hastily, "Miss Flora Payne, who sold us the house, said it had belonged to a niece of hers and some day she might come for it. So it ought not to be used. We'll put another blanket in your room today—this morning."

"We surely will," added Aunt Beatrice, with an undeniable air of having settled the matter.

And the blanket was on her bed before dinner time that noon. The patchwork quilt had been folded and put back into its carton, which in turn had been restored to the shelf in the closet. Ariel felt guilty; she would not have been surprised to find the closet locked, too; but it was not.

Nevertheless, in spite of the strange disapproval she had felt so strongly in her aunts—strange because they had indulged her since her childhood— she took the quilt out of its carton again that night and sat examining it. Its workmanship was exquisite, she saw at once. And it was quite obviously the work of but one hand—not the product of a quilting party— for the quality of the work was the same from one end of the quilt to the other. A labor of love, she decided— and felt that her decision was confirmed when she found, sewn in pink thread into one corner of it, up along the edge of a blue patch, the words Baby's Quilt. She concluded forthwith that the quilt must have been made for an undersized bed, not a baby's

179

bed exactly, but perhaps a child's bed, which explained in part why it had just barely served her the previous night.

She had already put the extra blanket on her bed, spreading it to her pillow; now, rather than fold the quilt, she laid it across the bottom of the bed against the possibility of even colder weather in the night. And, feeling thus fortified against any bitter weather, she opened the window a little, and stood for a moment there looking out to where the moon was rising, a waning moon, quite orange in that sky, with an unleafing tree silhouetted against it, and the few stones below it which belonged to the neighborhood cemetery.

How quiet and peaceful the country was! she thought again. And how welcome after months in the city! Save for the moon, all was dark except for a few yellow squares of windows, and in one place a light flowing from a barn. A dog barked, another answered far down the valley, a cow lowed, an owl hooted nearby—all else was still. And the house, too, was still, for her aunts had gone to their rooms well before her; perhaps they were already asleep.

She read for half an hour in a book of poems by Robert Frost and then yielded to her growing languor and went to bed. When the light was out, the pale glowing of the moon made a wan iridescence in the room, filling it with a personality it did not have under the clearer glow from the lamp. She lay for a little while contemplating the room, learning to "feel," as it were, the changed character of the room—the "guest" room, as her aunts had described it.

Under the moonlight, the room seemed to expand, and she, curiously, to seem smaller by comparison, and younger. How strange it was! It was a not

180

altogether unpleasant sensation to feel very young again, almost helplessly young, and she indulged it briefly before resolutely thrusting it from her thoughts and turning drowsily on her side to drift into sleep.

But she did not sleep as readily as she thought she might. The feeling of being young and helpless persisted, and with it came a sort of apprehension; it was nothing tangible, but only something that had a tenuous existence on the perimeter, as it were, of awareness, somewhere between the world of waking and the night of sleep, something that seemed to nag at her dispiritedly, not insistently, so that at last she was able to overcome it and close her eyes in sleep, shutting away the moonlit room and its odd character.

She started awake in less than an hour, and lay wondering what had awakened her. She lay quite still, senses alert, until she felt a movement at the foot of her bed. Then she turned her head slowly and cautiously.

In the room's reflected moonlight, she saw a woman bending over the bed, drawing the patchwork quilt up over the blankets.

"Aunt Ellen?" she murmured.

There was no answer.

She lay motionless. The woman was too slender to be Aunt Ellen, but not slender or tall enough to be Aunt Beatrice. And there was an indefinable quality of youth about her, too. Ariel could not see her face, but the moonlight did not glow there. She pretended to be asleep; the woman had evidently not heard her question; perhaps she was one of the domestics who "did" for her aunts, thought Ariel, though this would hardly explain her concern for the house guest.

The patchwork quilt came slowly, snugly up about

Ariel's shoulder; she could feel the woman tucking it into place around her. But it had been drawn up too high, up over her feet, almost to her knees, so that it was bunched on top of her, where it would certainly leave her too warm before the night was done. She had the impulse to straighten it, but refrained from doing so.

She strove to catch a glimpse of the woman's face, so that she might be able to identify her among the domestics; but there was only a moment when the woman looked down at her, the moonlight at her back, and then turned away, leaving Ariel conscious only of eyes that seemed to burn with longing, and a slight body as evanescent as the wind that had begun to billow the light lace curtains into the room at the window left open to the night.

Then the woman turned away and, though Ariel did not see the door open, for lying with her back to it, she knew intuitively that she was gone. She sat up and pulled down the quilt, then lay back and went wonderingly to sleep once more.

She woke again, past midnight, unbearably warm.

The quilt was back in place, bunched over her body.

She pulled it down once more, folding it loosely across the foot of the bed. Having now satisfied her most urgent need for sleep, she lay for a while on her back, waiting for sleep to overtake her again. Some of the moonlight had now withdrawn from the room, for the moon had risen higher, and only a small parallelogram of light lay under one window; though still airy, the room had grown darker and the foot of the bed was now shadowed.

It seemed to her presently that the shadows beyond the bed coalesced into one, and a vague apprehension stole into her awareness. She raised herself on her elbows, straining to look into the darkness, banishing the shadows. There was enough reflected light from this perspective to enable her to see that the door of the room was still closed, all the furniture was in its place, everything was as she had left it. Her apprehension washed away, and she lay back.

Almost at once, after she had composed herself, she felt a distinct movement at the foot of the bed. In a quick access of fear, she leaped from bed and reached for the lamp.

The patchwork quilt had been partly unfolded. It lay up along the bed by almost two feet further than she had left it.

She looked wildly around, her pulse racing. There was no one else in the room. In the soft lamplight, the room seemed almost naked in its ordinariness.

She stood until she grew aware of the chill air flowing in through the open window, looking unbelievingly at the patchwork quilt. Though her pulse subsided in the face of silence and the plainness of the room in the light of the lamp, her perplexity remained. How had the quilt moved? She had not touched it—nor had anyone else done so? She began to think that the quilt had a life all of its own, but the absurdity of this smote her and drove her at last to snatch up the quilt, fold it resolutely, and put it back into its carton, which she carried back to the closet and restored to the shelf where she had found it.

Nothing further disturbed her sleep.

In the morning she saw at once in the way her aunts looked at her when she came into the kitchen for breakfast that they waited on her words, afraid of what she might say. So they know something's the matter with that room, she thought. She said only

"Good morning!" as cheerfully as possible.

"Was the extra blanket enough to keep you warm, Ariel?" asked Aunt Beatrice.

"Oh, yes, thank you."

"You slept all right?" asked Aunt Ellen.

"Shouldn't I have?"

"Being at the southeast corner with cross-window circulation," put in Aunt Beatrice easily, "that room's subject to more temperature changes."

It did not sound quite reasonable to Ariel, so she only smiled and said nothing.

"Besides, it's the only guest room we have," said Aunt Ellen apologetically. "Of course, you could sleep in the parlor or the lounge," she added.

Aunt Beatrice interposed hastily. "Why on earth should she?" her manner formidably forbidding.

Aunt Ellen retreated meekly. "I only meant, if the room grew too cold."

Silence fell.

Ariel consumed a slice of toast. She felt the wary tension between her aunts as some sentient thing that had risen up to dominate the breakfast table. The silence grew oppressive.

"How many people help you here?" she asked presently.

"Oh, just two or three," said Aunt Ellen with manifest relief. "You know Mrs. Arons, who cooks for us. Then there's Johnson, who works outside—he's our hired man. And Mrs. Vickers comes in sometimes to 'do' the house for us."

"A small, slight woman?" asked Ariel.

"Yes, I guess you'd say she was that," said Aunt Ellen.

It was on the tip of her tongue to say "then it must have been she who came to tuck me in last night," but something in her Aunt Beatrice's intent gaze kept

184

the words unspoken. Instead, she said, "I should think it would be too much for just the two of you."

A few moments passed. Aunt Beatrice grew a little less tense.

"You said you bought this house from an old lady named Payne," Ariel ventured presently. "Is she dead?"

"Oh, no," said Aunt Ellen. "She's still alive. She must be eighty, wouldn't you say, Bea?"

"Yes, just eighty," said Aunt Beatrice.

"She lives down the road on that farm just across from the cemetery—her family cemetery it is, that little one on the knoll. The Paynes settled this valley two hundred years ago."

By degrees, the tension thawed and vanished. They spoke of Ariel's life in Portland, Maine, and of less prosaic matters, through breakfast and the morning.

Immediately after the noon meal, Ariel set out for a walk in the country. The day was pleasant; the autumn sun shone out of a clear sky and its light lay warmly on the leaves still clinging to the trees here and there, and on the sere grass in pastures and along the roadsides and woodlots. Her destination was Miss Flora Payne's house, but, so as not to seem obvious to her aunts, she went by a roundabout way and found herself presently in the cemetery on the knoll.

A stone wall that bounded it had broken down in three places. The tree Ariel had seen rose almost in the middle of it. The entire cemetery could not have been more than forty feet square, yet it was crowded with stones. She walked among them, reading the names now and then. *Josiah Payne, age 90— Hezekiah—Mary Fabor,* gathered in at but seven— *Abel Payne,* struck down in his middle years—*Rella Payne Fabor,* dead in her early twenties—*John*

185

Fabor, also dead in his early years—*Helen Payne*—*Marilla Payne Foster*—there were four or five generations of them represented in the little graveyard, which was bathed in an air of sweet melancholy, and which afforded the visitor a splendid view of the surrounding countryside, so that Ariel stayed long enough to look all up and down the valley and enjoy the rolling countryside so beautiful in the autumn sunlight, before she went down the slope toward the home of Miss Flora Payne.

The old lady was at home. She was a hawk-nosed, thin-faced old lady, very slight of frame, but evidently quite alert, for her eyes lit up at sight of company and she welcomed Ariel with patent delight. Ariel was not sure, but it seemed to her that a wariness came into the old lady's eyes when she learned who Ariel was and where she had come from.

Ariel was determined to give her no chance to put up her defenses, as her aunts had done. "They've put me into that room in the southeast corner," she said. "What happened there, Miss Payne?"

The old lady shook her head. "Ah, it's a sad house, Miss Bennett. It was originally my uncle's, but it came to his daughter. She lived there, and she died there—pined away, I expect you'd say. Her husband was killed—a runaway horse—such a young man too. Then little Mary took sick and died."

"In that room."

"Yes. And her mother lost her will to live after that. Seemed she couldn't wait to get up there on that hill with John and Mary."

"And the patchwork quilt you left there in the closet?"

The old lady gasped. "You've used it!" she said, accusingly.

"It was cold one night. There was no blanket," said

Ariel. "It shouldn't have been left there."

"I know. I couldn't bear to destroy it. Rella made it for her little girl. It's a beautiful quilt. But I couldn't take it with me, either—because—well, because the house was *uncomfortable* with the quilt, and I was afraid this one would be, too—wherever the quilt might be." She hesitated; then she asked, "Has the room been—*difficult* for you, Miss Bennett?"

"Not particularly."

"Because it seems to be just in that room—I suppose because Mary died there, under that quilt—I tried to figure it out, but I gave up at last. They've been dead ten or eleven years. A body'd think—in all that time—" Her sentence trailed off, unvoiced.

"You've never told anyone the room was haunted?"

"I've never said such a thing. *Is* it haunted, Miss Bennett? It's just the quilt that keeps coming up on the bed—you can't keep it off if you put it on the bed at all. I don't know what to make of it. I wish now— I've wished it often—we'd have done what Rella wanted—buried the quilt with her. It was such a crazy thing to ask and we all thought she was out of her mind."

Walking back down the road, Ariel thought she understood. The quilt had been bunched up on her in the night as if a child slept beneath it. All else was beyond her comprehension, and her entire experience required a suspension of disbelief which she was not entirely ready to concede. That she was not alone in this seemed to her evident in the curious hesitation everyone had in speaking about the house and the room and the patchwork quilt.

That night she took out the patchwork quilt and laid it at the foot of the bed. Then she put out the light and sat down to wait.

187

Once again moonlight flooded into the room, and the night wind blew, and the character of the room seemed to alter. She sat near the quilt at the foot of the bed, tense with apprehension, but firm in her determination. This time she would not be asleep or drowsy; this time she would see the woman who came.

From outside came the sounds of the countryside at night, rising, subsiding. The moon rose higher and the wind died down to a gentle breeze. The clock downstairs struck ten, then eleven. She began to feel a little absurd, and her tension thinned.

Then suddenly she was aware of a thickening of the shadows between the door and the bed.

The woman was there—the frail woman with the luminous eyes—coming toward the quilt.

Despite the quickening of fear that enveloped her, Ariel came to her feet, strode forward, picked up the quilt, and held it out.

"Here," she said. "Please take it."

She felt the patchwork quilt sliding from her hands.

In a few moments, the door of the bedroom opened and closed.

Ariel was alone. Her relief was so great that she stumbled to the bed and fell across it.

Next morning Aunt Beatrice asked anxiously how she had slept.

"Fine, when I once got to sleep," said Ariel. "I should tell you, though, that the patchwork quilt is gone."

"Gone!" cried Aunt Ellen. "Wherever did it go?"

"That 'someone' you mentioned came for it and I gave it to her," said Ariel.

A long minute of profound silence engulfed the breakfast table and everyone around it. Ariel expected that now, at last, her aunts would speak out, would admit what she herself could hardly deny.

But Aunt Beatrice only said, at last, "Well, it's a good thing. We're going to have a lovely day. There's a west wind blowing, and it's going to be warm."

Not another word.

By midmorning she began to wonder herself whether it had really happened.

The quilt was gone; there was no doubt whatever about that.

She was impelled by wild curiosity to walk to the cemetery on the knoll, and there, as she had feared, she found that something had disturbed the grave of Rella Payne Fabor. It looked as if something like a mole or a woodchuck.

The day was so pleasant that she stood for a few moments looking down in disbelief. She resisted the impulse to dig down a little to see what she could find. She was afraid of what might be there.

▪Fredric Brown

Nightmare in Yellow

He'd been a thief, and now he was going to become a murderer. Then his successful new life would start—successful as long as he kept to his timetable.

HE AWOKE when the alarm clock rang, but lay in bed awhile after he'd shut it off, going a final time over the plans he'd made for embezzlement that day and for murder that evening.

Every little detail had been worked out, but this was the final check. Tonight at forty-six minutes after eight he'd be free, in every way. He'd picked that moment because this was his fortieth birthday and that was the exact time of day, of the evening rather, when he had been born. His mother had been a bug on astrology, which was why the moment of his birth had been impressed on him so exactly. He wasn't superstitious himself but it had struck his

190

sense of humor to have his new life begin at forty, to the minute.

Time was running out on him, in any case. As a lawyer who specialized in handling estates, a lot of money passed through his hands—and some of it had passed into them. A year ago he'd "borrowed" five thousand dollars to put into something that looked like a sure-fire way to double or triple the money, but he'd lost it instead. Then he'd "borrowed" more to gamble with, in one way or another, to try to recoup the first loss. Now he was behind to the tune of over thirty thousand; the shortage couldn't be hidden more than another few months and there wasn't a hope that he could replace the missing money by that time. So he had been raising all the cash he could without arousing suspicion, by carefully liquidating assets, and by this afternoon he'd have running-away money to the tune of well over a hundred thousand dollars, enough to last him the rest of his life.

And they'd never catch him. He'd planned every detail of his trip, his destination, his new identity, and it was foolproof. He'd been working on it for months.

His decision to kill his wife had been relatively an afterthought. The motive was simple: he hated her. But it was only after he'd come to the decision that he'd never go to jail, that he'd kill himself if he was ever apprehended, that it came to him that—since he'd die anyway if caught—he had nothing to lose in leaving a dead wife behind him instead of a living one.

He'd hardly been able to keep from laughing at the appropriateness of the birthday present she'd given him (yesterday, a day ahead of time); it had been a new suitcase. She'd also talked him into celebrating

191

his birthday by letting her meet him downtown for dinner at seven. Little did she guess how the celebration would go after that. He planned to have her home by eight forty-six and satisfy his sense of the fitness of things by making himself a widower at that exact moment. There was a practical advantage, too, of leaving her dead. If he left her alive but asleep she'd guess what had happened and call the police when she found him gone in the morning. If he left her dead her body would not be found that soon, possibly not for two or three days, and he'd have a much better start.

Things went smoothly at his office; by the time he went to meet his wife everything was ready. But she dawdled over drinks and dinner and he began to worry whether he could get her home by eight forty-six. It was ridiculous, he knew, but it had become important that his moment of freedom should come then and not a minute earlier or a minute later. He watched his watch.

He would have missed it by half a minute if he'd waited till they were inside the house. But the dark of the porch of their house was perfectly safe, as safe as inside. He swung the blackjack viciously once, as she stood at the front door, waiting for him to open it. He caught her before she fell and managed to hold her upright with one arm while he got the door open and then got it closed from the inside.

Then he flicked the switch and yellow light leaped to fill the room, and, before they could see that his wife was dead and that he was holding her up, all the assembled birthday party guests shouted *"Surprise!"*